ANDROMEDA

By Julian Lechmus

ISBN 97809923037 8 5

Editor Dana McCown

Copyright © 2025 Julian Lechmus

StoryBridge Press

Brisbane, Queensland, Australia
2025

Cover design Dana McCown

PREFACE

It's a love story, but a bit different from all other love stories imaginable.

A strange refrigerator-like metallic box materializes on Jules' lawn. The door opens and out steps an amber- coloured creature that looks a tiny bit like a large octopus. It has eight long legs or arms that slither, slide and stand. It's got a thin, cylindrical body more like a very, very big bottle of beer, like one of those Northern Territory 60-litre specials bottles of beer, and it has four gorgeous, fluttering eyelids with lashes over large, round, purplish eyes. Jules is astounded and amazed, staring at the creature with his mouth agape, motionless and unable to utter a single syllable, let alone a word. Then, with what must be its mouth, as it has big red lips and is near the top of its body, it speaks. "Hey Jules, I meant to land in that USA institution called the *White House* and have some serious conversations with the current president whilst holding him up by his neck with only four arms, but I must have got the coordinates wrong, terribly wrong," it says in perfect English. It turns out to be a she, and she is rather entrancing.

And so, a new, captivating adventure begins, with many curves, bumps, and twists.

Embedded in the dialogue, the story does stretch the limits of satire, so it may not suit everyone. It is a political, scientific, and religious myth, as well as a satire of relationships, although the relationship aspects are genuinely heartfelt. Hope you enjoy and get a laugh.

Andromeda interjects, "Jules, I can see what you are writing, and you will have a postface, not a preface, if you write anything I do not approve of. You have to present me as highly attractive, highly intelligent, highly athletic, highly desirable and any other *highly* you can think of. Be careful, I'm watching you very carefully with all my four eyes."

"And who is this on the cover of the book you are writing about us? She has a human face but has eight arms and legs. She does not look anything like me. You better put a photo of the real me on the cover of the book, instead of an alien impersonator."

"Andromeda, it's for privacy reasons that your identity has to be kept a secret. You would find it quite intimidating if the paparazzi recognised you and hung outside our residence with cameras and microphones, hoping to get a camera shot of you and an interview, chase us at high speed if we go driving in our car, and possibly cause us to crash and die. We have to remain anonymous and safe."

"Jules, I may enjoy the attention and find it quite exhilarating, not intimidating." She then bursts out laughing and joins me by the computer desk for some serious writing with arms, legs wrapped around me and giving me kisses from all four sets of lips. Fantasy is so wonderful.

CHAPTER 1

After no luck on the RSPCA or is it the RSVP dating site, I joined the AlienSingles dating site and posted a profile. I included my address, planet Earth, and all the interstellar coordinates. I also said that I don't like travelling, as usually when I did, I contracted severe stomach problems and spent much of my time on the loo. I thought the post would be futile as I would have rotted in my grave, eaten by worms, by the time any eligible partner arrived from any distant exoplanet, but I was wrong.

She, at least I think it's a she, steps out of this fridge-looking device that materialized in my backyard. I look at her. She looks a bit like an Octopus, but with a cylindrical, reddish body, no chest-protruding appendages, eight arms or legs, and has a cute, cheeky smile, fluttering those very big four eyelids. She must be at least about 185 cm tall when standing upright, but then regresses to more of a slither along the ground. I'm kind of entranced. It's so weird, maybe she's into cosplay, and this is all some kind of an act or stage rehearsal.

"I just want to check you out. My name is Andromeda, and this dating scene can be dodgy. I met some sharks before on this site," she says in perfect English.

I don't think going for a coffee down the street would be a good idea, so I ask her to come inside. She slithers up the stairs.

"Where are you from?" I ask.

"A planet called Authentica and it's only 40 light-years away, so we're almost neighbours," she joyously replies while clapping her four hands.

"How did you get here so quickly? With our current spacecraft technology, it would take us many millions of years to go 40 light-years distance."

"Jules, that is your real name, I hope. We learned how to bend space, so we take shortcuts. I'll explain later," she says.

"What are those green things growing near where I landed?"

"They are called plants, and we eat some of them, well not all, not those tall plants which we call trees."

"We don't have them on my planet; how fascinating."

We do the customary one-hour dating site small talk chat, and then I guide her down to her fridge-like space-warping device to watch her departure.

She soon emerges from that device. "Jules, it will not start. The hyper-warpic resonator has burnt out. Can I stay here until I can source some parts to fix it, and do you have squids on this planet, as I am very hungry?"

She comes back inside and eyes my big LED TV. "Jules, it may contain the parts I need to fix my resonator."

"No way! That TV costs a lot of money on Earth, so wait till there's a kerbside hard rubbish collection; there are plenty of old TVs put out there to be collected for landfill."

"Can I stay?" she asks again, fluttering her eight eyelids. I reflect for a few microseconds.

"I have a spare bedroom you can use."

I place a motion sensor around my precious TV and attach a string to it, which is then attached to my left toe when I'm going to bed. It would wake me if she tried to fiddle with my TV in the middle of the night.

Months passed as we waited for the hard rubbish collection, and Andromeda is getting very thin. Cans of baked beans, the staple food of single guys, don't seem to provide her nutritional needs.

At first, we didn't talk too much, just watched TV. She once asked, "Are they real human people, those images on your TV device?"

One good thing about her, she's really quick at washing the dishes, mopping the kitchen floors, wiping the kitchen benches and vacuuming all at the same time. My house is spotless for the very first time ever. She'd be a hit in the hospitality industry, taking the jobs normally done by four people.

"Jules, can you get some squid for me? I don't like your attempts at heating cans of baked beans."

"I'm sorry, I'm a Baked Beanatarian, but how many squids do you want?"

"About 20, raw, not fried."

"Don't touch my TV set. I'll be back soon."

I hop in the car and drive to Harry's fish shop. I hope I have enough credit left on my Visa card.

"You must have many hungry visitors," Harry comments.

I return, barely able to hold four large bags of squirmy squid.

She slithers over to me and gives me a sort of kiss. She then opens the bags and goes into a feeding frenzy. I did offer some Soya sauce, but she was happy without any spices.

That night, she wanders into my bedroom. She appears to be shivering. "Jules, I am cold. I need some body heat. That electric blanket in the spare bedroom is interfering with my neural functions. Must be those electric fields that blanket gives out."

"Andromeda, I also give off electromagnetic radiation, EMR, as we call it. The EMR humans give off has a heating effect. We call it infrared radiation."

"Jules, I am so very cold, and I do not want to use that electricity blanket, and I also do not want a science lecture at the moment. Can I share the infrared heat radiation that your body emanates?"

Luckily, I have a Queen-Size bed, though I haven't washed the bedsheets for nearly a year. I usually just wait until they disintegrate and then buy new ones. This could be an incentive to *pull my finger out*, as they say in OZ, and tidy up my bedroom and get stuck into the linen washing and hygiene. I say yes, but I get a Texta colour pen and delineate the boundaries on the sheet that covers my mattress.

"That's your half and this is mine. My heat Electro Magnetic Radiation will travel and keep you warm." She doesn't believe that.

We're lying in my bed, but then she crosses the boundary. She wraps all her arms around me as she crawls in on my side of the bed. She ignored the boundaries. I hope the Texta pen lines on my bed sheets are machine washable.

"Jules, I have to be close to you. I'm not getting enough of that radiation from that distance." For a moment, I feel very cold, but it was only for a moment. I fall into a deep sleep. I hope she does too.

And so, a life-long relationship may have begun, maybe because I got the sledgehammer out and shattered to pieces any TV set in the kerbside hard rubbish collections. I have gotten used to having her around and want her to stay here on Earth with me.

"Jules, I think I found the part I need after taking apart your microwave oven," she says.

For a moment, I'm stunned, not about my microwave oven being dissected but about Andromeda leaving.

"Please don't go, don't go, don't go away, I'd like you to stay."

"Jules, I can return soon, but I've got a few things to tidy up back at home and see how my two or maybe three daughters are doing."

I give her a kiss as she steps into her refrigerator device, which soon vanishes. I feel despondent, but not for long. I went shopping to get a new microwave oven, and when I got back, the refrigerator-like device was in the back garden. She's waiting by the back door.

"What happened? I thought you'd be gone for a very long time."

"Do you want me to leave?"

"No, no, of course not; come inside."

"Jules, I spoke to my daughters and said they'd be welcome if they came to Earth. I hope you do not mind. Time works differently on our planet. We live close to a dying star that has a very large gravitational field that distorts time; it is like time lasts a lot longer, moves slower where we live. I was actually on my planet for the equivalent of 3 Earthian months. I will explain the physics later. Any fresh squid left over?"

"There is, but it's frozen. I'll defrost it, but don't touch this new microwave oven I just bought. By the way, I'm so glad you're back."

She slithers over and gives me a choking hug.

CHAPTER 2

My eight-legged or multi-armed friend from the *AlienSingles* dating site is becoming a bit bossy after she arrived back from her home planet.

This morning she orders me to go shopping and buy 10kg of squid. Of course, I couldn't take her with me, though the kiddies around the fish shop would have been amused, and the smartphone cameras would have been firing and overloaded as she hugs all of them at the same time.

When I got back home, Andromeda frantically devours 4kg of semi-frozen raw squid. I hope she doesn't eat humans, so it has me a bit worried, but she did an excellent job at cooking the rest of the squid for me to eat. The house is spotless; the bedsheets are washed, the beds are made, and the floors are sparkling clean.

Now I'm still worried when she wraps her eight arms around me as we watch the *Star Trek* TV series together. I gently move those arms away from my throat when there's a dramatic scene, and she gets excited.

But what if I didn't get the squid? Would I be next on the menu? She could certainly choke me with all those arms. Could I file for a domestic violence order and get government-funded compensation? These are serious questions we have to ask before we get involved with an alien species, but luckily, readers, I'm here to help and offer advice as I have learnt the practicalities and legal implications of alien involvement; just email me or go to my Internet site called *aliendatingadvice1000000.com.oz*. My rates are very reasonable.

"Andromeda, I was just joking when I said you could star in that *Star Trek* movie without having to put on makeup. Now, can you release your hands from my throat?"

"Jules, those squids you purchased were a bit off. I am going to have to vomit. Let me out to your garden. You must have chosen the left-over rotting supermarket dollar specials, you Earthian scunge bag", she says. I must admit I did, half-price on special at the local supermarket. Luckily, or in this case, unluckily, due to COVID-30, I have no sense of smell or taste, so I'll buy anything cheap, no matter how putrid it smells.

"I have to use your toilet," she says.

It's time to shut the bathroom door and turn the music up really loud as she uses all 8 to scuttle off to the bathroom. An hour later, she comes out of the bathroom looking rather blue in colour and somewhat thinner.

"Have you got a plunger device? Your toilet could not flush the contents that I exuded. It is blocked."

I rush down to the garage and bring up the plunger and a device with a flexible spring and a magnet that is only normally used if you accidentally drop your car keys down a crack in the floor or a toilet. The good or bad news is that my sense of smell has returned, so I must be free of the Covid virus. After an hour of plunging, I free up the toilet, and it flushes. It's given me an idea, though: invent an anti-smell mask. I'd make a fortune marketing it to parents of young children who need to perform constant nappy changing.

I ring Harry's Fish Shop. "Harry, do you deliver?"

"For orders over $200, we do."

"Harry, they've got to be fresh. Could I have $201 worth of raw squid?"

CHAPTER 3

Now, dear friends, you are probably wondering if Andromeda and I have ever done that intimate bedroom gymnastic stuff. I wouldn't even know how to start. There's nothing on Google on how to perform the act with an eight-legged alien who resembles an Octopus. Sure, we share the same bed, but she waves her eight arms when she's having a dream, and I end up being knocked off the bed only to resume sleeping on the floor, which is not that comfortable, but I'm getting used to it. But no, our relationship is purely platonic or Octopusic.

I also did some diligent research and looked at the stats. I have four limbs, and she has eight. That's 12 combined divided by 2, so any progeny would have, on average, six limbs. Would they be accepted into primary school? I don't know, but they could do any homework really quickly, writing several assignments at the same time.

Andromeda insists I remove my profile from the *AlienSingles* dating site, but today I got a wink from a *Celeste*. She only has six limbs and looks very sexy. I'm confused.

Andromeda slithers over. "Jules, you have to stop watching that stuff. Do not even think about that six-limbed creature. Eight are better than six, and you'd be doing much of the housework yourself. Your place was a mess before you met me, and I gobbled up all those overdue bill notices scattered all over your lounge room floor."

I turn off the computer, and once I find her mouth, 20 minutes later, I give Andromeda a kiss. Next day, there is a knock on the door. It's two very, very, very burly, threatening guys from a debt-collecting agency. Andromeda pounces on them, at their throats. She doesn't have fingerprints, so she doesn't have to wear rubber gloves like they usually do in TV crime series. I check their pulse afterwards as they are lying limply on the floor with a little bit of bleeding from their necks. They have weak pulses; it could have been just natural cardiac arrests after seeing Andromeda, but we can't take any chances. I ring the emergency health service hotline and request an ambulance for a life-or-death emergency.

"Andromeda, we don't attack people on Earth. Well, most humans don't, only those using a mind-altering drug called *ice* and some of our police and armies. We have to pack some stuff, all that we may need; we're going to be fugitives if those guys die. We're going to have to be on the run. You can probably move quicker than I can, so I'll hold on to you."

"Jules, I ran close to the speed of light when I was a wobbler in my home planet called Authentica; I got a Plutonium medal for my speed racing achievements, but I am much slower now. Don't worry. Did you buy more squid, or else I may have to eat you?"

Not a reassuring comment from Andromeda, but I think she has developed a sense of humour, at least I hope so. We rush out of the house, well at least Andromeda does. I'm riding on her, sort of like on her back, and holding onto her neck for my dear life as she accelerates. Eight legs are definitely quicker than two, four, or six. I hope that frozen squid I bought defrosts before she gets hungry, else I may end up on the menu.

And so, dear readers, a very dangerous but exciting journey begins.

CHAPTER 4

Guns start firing at us, the bullets travelling at over 300 km/hour. Andromeda slows down to sub-sonic speed and captures a few, which she munches. She must have a Lead or Copper deficiency. She continues skipping the waves whilst I, with a backpack full of supplies, hold on to her neck for my dear life.

I feel a bit sorry for the people we left behind. The sonic boom she generated must have shattered all their windows. Luckily, we plan to lead an inconspicuous lifestyle on a faraway island, so they won't be able to sue us for damages.

Andromeda would make the defunct Concorde supersonic jet appear like a wimp in the sky. It takes us less than 20 minutes to arrive on the island of Komodo, just off Indonesia. I'm covered in water and salty spray. We wait in the immigration queue and gather free food handouts.

We're third in line. First is a gigantic Komodo dragon lizard, and second is an exotic butterfly. Andromeda sends out her tongue and makes a very small meal of the butterfly. I restrain her from taking on the big lizard, even though it would be very popular on the UFC martial arts websites. Besides, I didn't bring my camera.

"Sir and madam octopi, what can I do for you?"

"Can we have a temporary visa for a few days?" I ask the immigration officer who is wearing eyeglasses with very thick lenses. He must be semi-blind.

"Sir, you can, but your two wives have to fill in these ten forms, and I do hope you are married. We don't tolerate any hanky-panky amongst unmarried beings in our country."

I whisper to Andromeda. "Are you up to it? Let's go to the Galapagos Islands instead."

"Let's go, Jules; I feel some indigestion after eating Madam Butterfly. I prefer to get moving quickly."

I check the food supplies, and they are almost defrosted.

"Andromeda, can we stop somewhere really hot on this journey? I'm getting really cold with all this wave skipping."

"Come over here, Jules, let me wrap all my arms around you. I will keep you warm, I promise; now is the squid defrosted?

And so dear friends, we jump continents, and I can barely hold on. We cause many massive sonic booms and leave a trail of mass destruction. City buildings tremble, boats sink, and villages are destroyed. That *Conald T* guy declared a state of emergency, believing his country was under attack. He was, however, restrained from launching nuclear warheads at China, Russia, Ukraine and Eskimo-inhabited nations.

Andromeda must have built-in GPS. We quickly reach our destination, one of the more secluded Galapagos Islands. Andromeda dives into the ocean, and when she comes up, she has a mouth full of sea creatures and is smiling—no need to cook tonight. I munch on a bit of raw squid and berries whilst watching her dive again and again. At this rate, she'll become fat. It seems like there is a lot of food here, which is very reassuring as it means that I may not end up on the menu.

CHAPTER 5

"Andromeda, I'm getting bored here, and you're eating far too much."

It's not diplomatic to say that to an alien woman with eight arms and knuckles, or in fact to any woman.

"I'm bleeding profusely."

"I'm sorry, Jules. I didn't mean to hit you that hard. Your Earthian blood will soon coagulate, so you will stop bleeding."

I cautiously lift my head.

"Jules, I have a wireless Internet router built into my anatomy and can interpret electrical signals. I also follow the news your planet produces. We are going to need a Tax haven. See these over 10,000 pearls I nearly spat out when eating shellfish, but I kept them. They are worth a fortune on your planet, and if we sell them, we could get a freshwater swimming pool built so you could go swimming with me, as you appear to be allergic to seawater."

"Andromeda, the nearest Tax haven is the Cayman Islands; many big companies have their unoccupied headquarters there and redirect all their mail and email back to their mainland."

"Jules, I'm just checking. The Caymans are only a hop, skip and a jump away, and as you implied, many of their headquarters are not occupied. We would not interfere with their mail and their redirection services. We could live a life of opulence rather than sleep on this beach where I constantly have to protect you against the crabs that come crawling out of the ocean at night, though they do taste good when I catch them, and they are low in calories."

"Andromeda, what are the alternatives?"

"Jules, you could come to my planet, Authentica, though you may not survive the hyperspace journey, and we don't have that much oxygen there. But you would make a good museum specimen in the *Department of Unnatural Planetary History*."

The choices are not that great. I prefer to stay on Earth.

"OK, I'll pack the pearls into my backpack, and we'll go to the Caymans. I'm sure we can sell them there and not be slugged with a tax bill. Let's go."

And so I mount Andromeda, in the way you mount a bicycle or horse—nothing inappropriate. It's a 10-minute journey, and after causing many more sonic booms and again destroying many island villages, we arrive. Andromeda can pick any lock, so we are in a luxurious abandoned apartment. She wraps her eight arms around me. "Not my neck, Andromeda; I do need oxygen."

"Jules, I did sustain a slight injury on one of my arms when I was collecting seashells on the sea floor. I was attacked by one of your Great White sharks. I came out better off than the shark did. I took a nibble, well maybe a large bite, but it didn't taste as good as the shellfish and squid, so I didn't drag the shark to shore."

"Are you OK? What's that purple stuff coming out of arm number 7? Is it the equivalent of our human blood? You should have told me earlier. I would have found some seaweed to wrap around the wound."

"It is OK, Jules, relax; I heal quickly; it is just an insignificant wound."

We fall asleep, and I don't get eaten, not just yet. Just to make sure it never happens again, I'll sell the pearls tomorrow and buy a fishing fleet of boats, not to sell the produce but to keep Andromeda's calorie intake satisfied.

CHAPTER 6

The fishing fleet we purchased came in late to shore and didn't properly refrigerate their catch. Needless to say, it's not a nice experience when an alien octopus-like creature vomits its guts over me. Luckily the shower works.

Andromeda rushes at the sea captain and nearly rips him apart. I had to stop her as best as I could.

"Andromeda, calm down; life is not just about food; you nearly killed that guy."

"Jules, I'm just trying to adjust to this planet. Not much makes sense to me here. We don't have wars or any unscrupulous dealings on my planet. Food always arrives on time, is fresh, and we have no need for debt collectors or insurance policies; we are totally ethical, unlike what seems on this planet."

I prefer to say but desist, for my life's sake, that moving to the Cayman Islands was not totally ethical.

"Jules, my arm is healed. We can be like *Bonnie and Clyde*. I never did watch the whole movie as TV reception was pretty bad by the time it got to my planet 40 light-years away, but maybe we can watch it now."

"No, Andromeda, we're not going to be fugitives all our lives. You have to restrain your behaviour, else I'll have to chain you up in chains and steel ropes."

"That could be fun, Jules, but the chains better be made from platinum, or else I'll chew through them."

"OK, let's run for it, or you do, and I'll hold on. We still got wads of cash in Cayman currency."

An old Beatles song comes on the radio – *'I'd like to live under the sea, in an octo….'*. I switch the radio off. "We've got to get going, somewhere on Earth where there are no humans, and we don't have to utilise any diplomatic skills."

"How about that island called Madagascar? I read it has got yummy, colourful lizards. I might become a reformed sea-life dependent and instead a lizardatarian," she says.

"OK, let's go. The backpack is packed."

I grab hold. The sonic boom destroyed most of the tax haven properties on the Cayman Islands, so we're not doing other countries' companies any tax-dodging favours.

"Jules, what about this spot? There are no humans around, but plenty of lizards. I'll build us a hut, and you can help."

And so, a new adventure begins.

PS: Dear readers, no exotic protected lizards were harmed or consumed. There is a local Fish&Chips shop nearby, well not really nearby, a few hundred kilometres (70 seconds away at the speed Andromeda travels). Luckily, we had plenty of pearls left to pay the shop owner, as that Cayman currency is worthless. I held on tight, holding 100 kg of seafood goodies, and fortunately, Andromeda doesn't mind salt and a lot of vinegar. "I love this vinegar liquid made from decomposed vegetables; I will email the recipe back to my planet." She says. So, a life of *Fish&Chips* begins.

CHAPTER 7

I return from a brief exploratory walk of the landscape. I walk into the hut, shake my head and rub my eyes. I am seeing double or triple, no quadruple. Must have been those mushrooms I picked and ate.

They all look alike. Andromeda slithers over to me. "Jules, that is my mother, and those are my two sisters. You will not be able to pronounce their names. Just call them *Mum*, *S1* and *S2*."

"Andromeda, do they taste good on this planet, his kind, I mean," asks Mother as she, licking her lips, points at me with all eight arms. I feel like running for my life.

"Mother, they do not do that sort of thing on this planet, eat males I mean, but how did you get here so quickly?"

"Darling, we got the hyperdrives working again and picked up the hyperspace email you sent and the recipe for that tasty liquid you call vinegar. We could not brew enough of it, so we traced your location. Now, can you pour some of that vinegar on him? We're hungry after the journey."

The two sisters are also licking their lips and tongues in anticipation. This is like a moment in your life when, even if you're an atheist, you start praying.

"Mother, why did you and my sisters really come here to this planet?"

"Darling, our fresh seafood supplies have dried up. We over-fished, so we had to eat the males of our species despite the fact that they were quite small in size and tasted terrible. They are all gone, so we thought we would try this world because you are here, and there is a substantial male population, 4 billion to choose from and keep our appetites satisfied. We are not detectable by this planet's space agencies; we have cloaking devices on our craft, so we cannot be traced, so you are safe, my darling."

"Mother, there are plenty of fish and crustaceans here. You and my sisters do not have to eat any humans; besides, they taste really, really bad. You'd be vomiting and pooing all night long."

"OK darling, what else have you got to eat?"

Nervously, I drag out the huge Esky fridge filled with goodies from the *Fish&Chip* shop. "Have you got more vinegar?" one of the sisters yells. I bring out a bottle of freshly prepared vinegar. A feeding frenzy follows, and all 100 kg of seafood is devoured within minutes. The Authenticans definitely don't have any table manners.

"Yum," one of the sisters says, and the others follow with the yums.

"Andromeda, I don't think our fragile planet can cope with your relatives unless they become vegetarian," I whisper to her.

"Jules, if we became vegetarians, we'd devour your rainforests or what is left of them within hours. We have to think of another solution."

The mother and sisters are lying on the floor, digesting and, need I say, exhuming lots of gases from wherever their exit passage is. For a moment, I thought of lighting a match and running as fast as I can. The methane must be affecting my brain.

"Put away that match. It would not do any good anyway. We will find another solution," Andromeda says.

I go to sleep on the hammock that we found on the beach and which I strung up between two trees. The mosquitoes are getting a good feed, but it's better than being inside, and those alien octopi eating me.

I awake and can hear the conversation.

"Darling, are you going to do it? I mean the reproductive act. You might produce a new species, and you would make it to the *Hall of Fame* back on our planet. We could clone him, and the male kids you produce could provide us with an endless four-legged food supply."

"Mother, our relationship is not like that. Besides, his reproductive organ is very short, not like that of the males who once lived back on Authentica, which you ate and exterminated."

"Darling, I am sure they have surgeons on this planet that can extend his down-under piece to 500cm."

"Mother, enough! He's not a horse. Go to sleep and tell my sisters that nibbling Jules is forbidden, even if they get hungry at night, or else I will eat them. I'm stronger than they are and have a bigger appetite."

Andromeda slithers over to my hammock and wraps all her eight arms around me. "I will not let them consume you despite your deficiencies," she assures me.

"Andromeda, not the throat; I told you that before!"

The thought very briefly crosses my mind on how to live with a potential mother-in-law around and the other ravenous siblings. I hope our oceans are full of seafood and there are no surgeons around to extend me. My mind wanders again, but sorry, it's XXX rated, I'm happy with what's down under the pants.

"Andromeda gives me a very, very slight nibble on my left toe as it's very sore after I dropped the exercise dumbbell on it. I ask. "Please stop, I didn't mean that you try to eat my toe. She complies, and I feel just a tiny bit of pain. This situation, at the moment, just seems to be a really bad dream.

CHAPTER 8

I rub my eyes after I fall out of the hammock.
"What are you doing, Andromeda?"
"Jules, I am recalibrating the hyperdrive."
"But why Andromeda? I think I can handle, well, not handle, but I could possibly cope with your family being here on Earth."

"Jules, we have to return back home as we have no immunity to viruses and your planet seems to have a particularly nasty one at the moment."

"Can I help? I'll miss you. Will you return when we get rid of this Novel Coronavirus, and we have a vaccine that works on aliens as well? It's only those anti-vaccinators that will delay things."

"Jules, nothing personal, but I like those pictures of the virus even though they appear to have more arms than our species does."

"Andromeda, will you come back to Earth again?"

"I will, Jules, providing I can get this hyperdrive fixed again; it has become temperamental. Else, if I come back at normal speed, you will be in a rotting coffin and being eaten by your earthworms instead of me." She must have read my mind.

I come over to Andromeda and repeat again, "I'll miss you."

She slithers over to me and gives a long passionate tongue kiss. I nearly choke as she has a very long, thick tongue, and it blocks my airways, so I'm coughing and spluttering, trying to get air.

The rest of her family come out rubbing their multiple eyes.

"Jules, you can speed up my return, but you have to sneak into an ICU that houses infectious Corona patients. Pretend you are a doctor. I can print an ID that you can wear around your neck. Wear a facemask and tickle a patient to get them to splatter some saliva into this sample jar. We can then develop a vaccine far quicker than you humans can, but unfortunately, it may only work for our species."

Andromeda gives me a ride close to Melbourne City where currently there are many infectious cases. I walk into the Alfred Hospital, displaying my nametag and reassuring the receptionist that I'm a visiting doctor. "Floor three is COVID-19++ infectious diseases," the receptionist says, "but you better wear a mask. You can have this one". I wipe the sweat from my face. So far, I've pulled it off.

I tickle the foot of one of the COVID-19++ patients after I disconnected him from the life-support system. He's bursting out in laughter and splattering saliva, and soon fills the sample jar. Much later, it was discovered that laughter was the best medicine for those suffering lung infections, and the guy made a full recovery.

"Andromeda, here is the vial full of spit and splutter."

"Jules, I read the newspapers from back in your home city. Those two guys who suffered what you call myocardial infarctions were diagnosed as consuming multiple pharmacological substances, many illegal, before that incident. You may have to give a police statement, but their demise has nothing to do with you or me. You may have to give a sworn police statement. Just say you panicked when you ran away. We should go back to your hometown of Brisbane when I get back."

"Mum and Sis, we have to leave this world if we want to live, or else we'll be consumed by a tiny, microscopic virus till we find a vaccine. Jules, do you want a lift back to that country you call OZ? It won't take long, and you can keep the remaining pearls."

"Andromeda, one of our sun's planets, *Saturn*, has a moon called *Enceladus* with an atmosphere of methane, ice, and lots of water below. There may be yummies to catch there."

"Jules, we'll stop to check it out. Now take care."

"Andromeda, I'll take the offer of a lift back home, but please come back soon using the hyperdrive, as I take pride in my appearance and don't particularly cherish the thought of being consumed by earthworms."

"If I don't make it back soon, get a cremation. Now hold on. Taking off can be a bit of a rough ride."

I check my clocks back home in Brisbane. Only 20 minutes have passed, which seems like an eternity. I still have time to pay all those overdue bills, which I got off the Internet after Andromeda ate the original paper copies. I ponder whether her device sent us back in time. There were no articles in the newspapers about debt collectors dying or us escaping police apprehension.

I get a hyperspace email. *'Jules, my mother and sisters love this Saturn moon called Enceladus, which is full of goodies 5 km below the surface of ice, but I miss you. Send me an email so I can get your current coordinates. Love, Andromeda.'*

I do and email *'Wish you were here'*.

I spend the nights looking at the sky, then a flash appears, and the fridge-like device materializes in my kitchen.

Out slithers Andromeda, without the other hungry relatives. "Mum and my sisters say you have passed the test. They love *Enceladus* and all the seafood delights."

I relax. I can now stop eating a jar of crushed garlic a day to make myself unpalatable.

"Andromeda, aren't you worried about being back in this virus-infested world?"

"It is OK, Jules. We have developed a vaccine, but as I said before, it only works for our species. You still have to be careful. I brought some facemasks back. You should wear one."

"Andromeda, I'm so glad you're back, but I don't think these face masks are designed for Earthlings. I try to imagine taking Andromeda to the local pharmacy or doctor for the vaccine shot. It will cause more panic in the streets than any virus and probably cause more deaths than the virus, as citizens and young kids rush away and don't stop when the pedestrian crossing lights are red."

Maybe I can find a long hood that extends to the floor and put a mask over her head.

I try to give her a kiss, but can't find her mouth, so I just wrap my only two arms around her. She does the same, but nearly chokes me.

"Jules, I'm hungry. Have they got one of those *Fish&Chips* shops where you currently live?"

"Andromeda, we're back at my house in OZ. Have you forgotten? The shops are opening soon, but I've hoarded a stockpile of vinegar, frozen seafood, and toilet paper, so we don't have to do any shopping for at least a day or two." I briefly wonder if all this space travel can induce confusion or premature dementia. She rubs her head with all eight arms.

We're sitting on the couch watching the news on TV. Andromeda comments, "I could eat that *Trumpsy* guy and do your planet a favour."

"Andromeda, forget about that idea. You'd be vomiting for months and clog up the whole sewerage system in this country."

That's life; it's never simple, well at least not on Earth. I've got the radio on. That ancient *Beatles* song comes on again – 'I *want to live under the sea in an octopus's garden ...'*. Can't the ABC radio channel play music that is more contemporary? Maybe they're cost-cutting due to funding cuts. I let the song finish.

Andromeda slithers over and says, "I like that song". I hyper-ventilate for a few minutes before exhaling and give her a hug. She reciprocates, squeezing me tightly. My lungs are safe because I learnt the exhaling trick, but my eyeballs are ready to pop out.

CHAPTER 9

Just as Andromeda was getting used to eating cow and lamb meat, the *T. Abbott* abattoirs closes down, so we can't get any meat protein, though plenty of bullshit, which is really good for the veggie garden that I'm trying to start. So life continues.

"Andromeda, the vaccine you manufactured may not last, especially if the virus mutates. You should still be afraid of this virus sweeping our planet."

"No Jules, I traded some of the pearls you had left to buy this special light lamp from one of your alternative health gurus and ex-media cooks, called *Pete*. It generates waves that are supposed to protect us against the COVID-19++ viruses. It only cost $15k worth of pearls, and I'm bathing in its light just as you speak."

Andromeda and I wander to the Brisbane River late at night. She has the full-body hoody garment and a full-face mask called a burkha on, with only two of her eyes visible. We passed a gentleman with a lot of facial hair hanging from his chin and neck who asks if Andromeda would like to join the

Muslim community. She politely declines. Andromeda then strips off and jumps into the river. Before no time, she throws a Bull shark in my direction. I eventually manage to pick it up despite the 1.5m shark furiously wiggling and whipping and causing more than just a nibble on my arms. We slither back to my place, Andromeda carrying me and the now-dead shark. A trail of blood is left behind, my blood.

I look behind. Luckily, a wild dog, possibly a Dingo, is licking the blood off the footpath, so we won't get traced by the police.

"Jules, have you got some bandages, a needle, and thread? I will suture your wounds and stop your bleeding."

"Yes, in the bathroom, but be quick."

And so, whilst trying not to scream in pain or due to the bad smell of one of my very smelly socks in my mouth, I get sewn up by Andromeda, and the bleeding stops. No neighbours were woken. She licks the blood from my arms and says yum, definitely a potential worry.

A few days pass. It will be another night of *Flake* fish from the local Fish&Chips shop (they deliver) with lots of vinegar, till Andromeda modifies her diet again so I don't have to face any more injuries from fish with sharp teeth.

I ask her as we lie curled in bed, "Andromeda, could we review this concept of becoming vegetarian again?"

"Jules, I told you before, our species needs the calories to keep our eight legs mobile. You would have to buy 1000kg a day of the vegetable matter and a lot more vinegar to make me stomach those greenies."

"Andromeda, I've talked to the local Fish&Chips owner. He'd be really happy if we could pick up the lard and oils from the cooking. It's full of calories and smells of fish."

"Jules, you appear to have done your research. I will consider that. Now, can we make love? I found a 2-metre piece of garden hose in your shed. You can connect it to extend yourself."

The very thought of extending myself with garden hose irks me. Talk about a weird relationship. There was no extending or inserting wherever that may be. We just fell asleep curled up, and she doesn't go for my throat.

CHAPTER 10

Needless to say, dear friends, we didn't perform the bedroom gymnastics that night or any other night or day, even though by Earth years, we've been together for a very long time. I had Googled *Authentican women* and apparently, they're kind of like our spider species, not only because they have eight arms, but they also consume their partner after the mating act. I'm staying a virgin, well, at least with the alien-species kind.

I get up early and walk to the flower shop to buy Andromeda some flowers, as she's feeling a bit down and missing her home world. While walking, I bump into Mildred, an old girlfriend of mine—oops, not that old, just previous. We chat briefly, but she slips her business card with contact details into my pocket. I should have destroyed that card.

"Jules, I am doing the washing, something you have not done in eons, as your clothes and bed sheets exude an unpleasant odour. Take off those pants. What is this, a card from a Mildred? I will tear you apart and eat you if you are cheating on me."

I hand her the flowers, and Andromeda gobbles them up instantly. So much for putting flowers in a vase. Maybe she's getting into vegetarianism, but the flower bill would be horrendous.

I try to find her mouth and kiss her. "I love you, there's only you," I say.

Another twenty Earth years have passed, and my greying hairs are starting to fall out. Andromeda still looks the same and is knitting four jumpers at the same time while we watch some very old episodes of *Star Trek*, her favourite Earthian TV show.

"Jules, I like the TV show, but it has very many scientific flaws."

"Andromeda, that TV show is about relationships, not science.

"Jules, could you get some sump oil out of that car that you have not used for years or changed its oil? I am sure the oil is black, and you could colour your hair, so you do not appear so aged. You could call the recipe Grec...2000, no, that name has already been taken, so how about Bris4000?

I try Andromeda's suggestion and have dark motor oil dripping from my hair down to my face. I hope it's not carcinogenic. She comes over to me and wipes it all over my face and other parts of my body.

"Jules, you may become eligible for some government disability payments called NDIS. Just do not get the turps out too soon and appear too young, as we are running out of pearls, and Jules, you look like one of those sexy dark-skinned guys, though deficient down under. Now stop vicariously indulging with those young Earth women on that Internet site that you watch when you think I am asleep."

"Andromeda, it's not like that. I'm just doing psychological scientific research on the topic of *Male Dependence on Media for Gratification*."

"Stop pulling my leg, any 8 of them," she replies.

I cuddle up next to her as we watch TV, and I look at her. To me, she is beautiful. I also email her mother, who's still frolicking and eating all the fish-type life on Saturn's moon.

"Jules, the gravity on Earth is far stronger than on Authentica, and you have a hundred times more oxygen in the atmosphere. I'm oxidising and getting prematurely old, almost as old as you," Andromeda says.

"Andromeda, you have certainly aged, but do you want to try that garden hose extension again? I might give it a try?"

"Jules, you are too old by this planet's standards, but we can have a cuddle. I'll never leave you until you are dead from natural causes, and then I will eat you so that you become part of me, well, the part I don't excrete."

She has such a reassuring way of expressing herself. I give her a hug, and we continue watching *Star Trek*. All is well, and she likes my new black hair and motor oil body odour.

"Mm, that used motor oil smells so good," she says.

Then her mum materialises and slithers over to Andromeda. "Darling, are you alright? You have aged thousands of years. If you want, I can decimate this human who is making you grow so old."

"Mum, we are happy together. Please do not eat him. We love each other in a non-earthly sort of way."

The mother looks at me sternly. "You better keep on looking after my daughter."

Then she moves closer. I'm about to make a run for it, but she grabs me. "You have looked after my daughter well, and she seems happy. When is the wedding? I can get the hyperdrive going again, and we can all be here within a week, Earth time, all 30 of us close relatives."

I'm briefly trying to think, do I know any male Octopi that don't mind being consumed?

The mother read my mind. "Jules, we do not eat males anymore, just ask any male friends to the wedding if you have any. There will be 30 females of our species arriving soon so order plenty of seafood and vinegar, else we may revert to our previous dietary habits. I hope you do not end up being a dud like the 10 other husbands Andromeda had in the past."

"I just hope I don't end up on the menu," I reply in a scared-sounding voice.

The mother kisses her daughter ever so gently. The mother then gives me a gentle hug before she leaves and hops back into hyperspace.

I grab Andromeda with my only two arms. "Will you marry me?" I ask.

"Where are the eight wedding rings? In our culture, you have to have one for a finger on each arm?" Moments later, which seemed like an eternity, she replies, "I will, and then giggles; I was pulling your foot as they say on this planet."

"So, you won't marry me?"

"Of course, I will. I meant the eight wedding rings. I possess 160 from previous marriages; I do not need any more. I will send a hyperspace email to Mum to get the girls to bring back the rest of the rings. We will sell them as we are down to the last pearl, and the food bill, thousands of kilograms of seafood for the wedding, will shock you."

Something doesn't make sense. 160 divided by 8 makes 20 former husbands. I Google; it doesn't break the Earthian record held by a Baptist preacher who had 23 wives (not concurrently). I should have focused on religious studies while at university.

"What if I take you down the coast and you do some deep-sea diving and get some more oysters? Some will have pearls which we could sell."

"Jules, I do not think I can do deep-sea diving anymore. Why don't you get a job to pay for the wedding in case my daughters don't bring the gold wedding rings? You have not worked since I have known you."

All sorts of justifications come flooding into my mind for my slackness. "There are no jobs in my line of work out here in Brisbane. Besides, I have tried. All that time I was on the Internet, I was mainly searching the job sites."

"Jules, you are too old to be a gigolo or whatever it is called. We will just sell the rings. Besides, I like you being at home, but in the future, stay away from those dubious websites."

I come over to her and give her a hug. "Andromeda, do the women wear wedding gowns on your planet? If they do, I'll purchase a sewing machine, and you can make one."

"No Jules, we are totally, what is the word on your planet, we perform the ceremony totally naked."

Oh gawd, I'll have to check in the mirror and make sure the sump oil is evenly distributed. I give her a kiss and go outside to the swimming pool, where it is sunny and I can inspect myself. I haven't put any chemicals in it for over 30 years or drained it. The water is green, covered with thrashing algae and other creatures. For a while, my mind wanders. Should I drain and clean it? No, on second thought, the wedding guests will do that.

Chapter 11

A few days pass and I frantically ring Harry, who is the owner of the local *Fish&Chips* shop. As his best-paying customer, we've developed some trust, and he doesn't ask too many questions.

"Harry, this is a strange request, but can you contact your mates who run deep-sea fishing boats. I need 30 live, large male octopuses."

"Jules, I can't tell their gender. They all look the same to me."

"OK Harry, tell your friends to catch 60 of them; chances are half will be male, and they will probably be returned alive so you can cook those great calamari meals. Harry, it's nothing weird; it's just a documentary I'm making for ABC TV about our sea friends."

"Jules, that will cost more than a bit; a refrigerated truck. Have you got the cash?"

"No, but I will have gold rings to pay you with, and after all, we're moving into a cashless economy."

"Jules, those octopuses eat a lot. You may need an extra 4000kg of seafood."

"That's fine, Harry, just source the necessary supplies and deliver them. I can't pick them up as I'm planning my wedding in a week's time."

"Jules, I won't ask any further questions as I'm bound by *the fish supplier's confidentiality code.*"

Four burly guys, using wheelbarrows, manage to get the Octopi into my backyard pool and deliver the extra seafood. It took six hours for them to do the unpacking; I'll hate to see the bill.

The Octopi revive and go into a feeding frenzy. All the green algae is gone, and the pool looks spotless and doesn't need any cleaning on my part.

Andromeda slithers over to me. "I'm sure my daughters and cousins will enjoy the company in the pool. Now you have to get undressed. All guests and participants have to be naked to partake in our culture's marriage ceremony.

"I told you before. I'll be embarrassed exposing my private parts."

"Don't worry, Jules. No one will see your private parts unless they have an electron microscope with them."

Before I have a chance to pull down my pants and reassure the female audience that I am endowed enough and fully functional, the hyperdrive flashes again. The 30 Authentican Octopi girls come in waving alien gifts, along with Andromeda's mother, who definitely isn't part of the gifts.

The mother gives me a reluctant hug, "Look after my daughter," she whispers. "Now, have you got the eight gold wedding bands required for the ceremony?"

"No, I don't. We won't wear gold rings or bands, but we have tattoos painfully sculpted on our backsides or bottoms that say, 'I'm taken, can you see?' Our faces would be hideously scarred if we tried to surgically remove them and indulge with somebody else."

She bows, "I accept you as my son-in-law."

I bow as well.

"I promise I will, rain, hail, snow, or if our planet runs out of squid, I'll be there for her," I whisper back to my future mother-in-law, and then she gives me another bear hug or octopus hug, same thing. I guess I'm approved to be sort of an octopus.

"Jules, just say you like the gifts, Andromeda whispers. You can always donate unwanted gifts to the charity shop afterwards. I read that everyone does that on your planet, or puts them on that eBay website and sells them."

I walk over to all the Octopi girls and give them a hug with my limited two arms. I wish I had sixty arms so we could get that over sooner. My ribs hurt.

"Girls, just jump into the pool, the food will be ready soon, so don't eat anyone."

One of the Octopi ladies looks at me and says, "He smells so good". It must be the motor oil, which I haven't fully washed off yet.

There are squeals of joy coming from the pool. For a moment, I get worried. With the COVID-19++ isolation rules, we're only allowed 10 human visitors. Well, if the neighbours call the police, there's only one human here, so we should be right. I look at the beautiful Andromeda. "How fast can these fillies run? We got this race in Melbourne called the

Melbourne Cup. The first prize would mean I'd never have to work again or look for a job."

"Jules, they have eight legs or arms, so they may have a double unfair advantage over the competition, but I will ask them."

The alien preacher is part of the congregation. "I pronounce you something and something; now you can kiss the bride." I do that once I find her mouth.

Well, dear friends, we are as wealthy as can be as three of the filly Octopi stepdaughters stayed on Earth with us and have won many horse races, including the most prestigious Melbourne Cup. First, second and third, even though we had to duct tape half their legs together just to let them qualify and give the horses an even chance.

I ring Harry, "The usual mate, 1000kg of seafood and lots of vinegar. Oh, and can I borrow one of your delivery vans again? I'll pay $1 per kilometre as usual."

"Jules, I hope you're not some kind of drug courier because I don't approve of that."

"Harry, if I was, I'd be driving a Porsche car. It's just that my very big wife and I like to go for an occasional drive and watch the horse races." Luckily, Andromeda did not hear that last comment.

"Well OK," Harry replies,

The girls are frolicking in the pool and later say goodbye to their 60 friends, and along with Andromeda's mum, they enter the hyperdrive and vanish, but only temporarily. They will be back.

I look at Andromeda and hold one of her hands while we rock in the chairs, watching the sunset. Andromeda says, "The three remaining Authentican fillies, who couldn't fit into the hyperdrive, are my daughters from a previous marriage. I can't remember which one, and they haven't even reached puberty yet. That happens when they will be equivalent to 1,000 Earth years on Authentica, but may occur much sooner on your planet. They will go wild once the hormones kick in. You would not be able to cope with only two hands when they get older. I'm ringing Mum; I hope she can use the hyperdrive to take them back home. Jules, the connection is not working. I can't reach mum," She frantically yells.

"It's Ok, they can stay if they want to."

And so when I thought it was all over, we got 3 alien female teenagers to look after. Still, they keep on winning races and boosting our financial coffers. I walk downstairs to where my now three octopi stepdaughters sleep. I kiss them all gently once I find a spot. I walk back upstairs. I forgot to turn the radio off. A song called *"What If God Was One of Us"* *comes on,* soon followed by *"If God Smoked Cannabis"* by the same artist, Joan Osborne. I sort of relate to those songs. I give Andromeda a kiss before falling into bed and wrapping my arms around her.

And so, an extra new adventure begins, bringing up teenagers, a harder task than anything I've ever encountered before.

Chapter 12

After a week, I am half trying to drain the pool. The girls and the other 60 Octopi are back frolicking in the semi-drained pool. The hyperdrive must have broken down again, and that's why they're all back. I have no idea if any Octopanky activities occurred. They just play ball games. trying to score goals in the nets I had set up. Finally, Harry's behemoth guys, whom he hired, come over with wheelbarrows to pick up the Octopi, one by one.

"Guy's not that one, she's one of my wife's daughters."

"Man, you're weird," he replies.

"What's going to happen to them?" I ask.

"Don't know, mate. Ask Harry, he's the marketing guy, but I guess they'll end up in fish markets."

I ponder. Well, at least they had a good time before they ended up on a dining room table.

One of Andromeda's daughters slithers over to me in a very menacing way. "Why did you let them take my friends away? We were having such a good time."

"Kid, I don't know. I made a bad mistake. We humans make heaps of bad mistakes. I'm so very, very sorry. I should never have done that. Can you forgive me?" She gives a snarl back. I never felt so bad in my life. Just sentenced 60 friends of my stepdaughters to end up on a restaurant menu.

I'm finally back on the computer, feeling like shit. A song starts playing on that YouTube channel. I'm listening again to that song by that music group called *MGMT* and the song called *Kids*. Andromeda comes over with a big glass of water. "You got to stop listening to that song. You are losing a lot of water through all those tears, you will dehydrate."

I log onto a web-purchasing site. I purchase 4 veils (3 for the girls and one for Andromeda so she doesn't have to wear that COVID-19++ protection mask to hide her face, which would really make her look like an alien. I'm also purchasing long colourful gowns, shoulder to floor, for all of them. After all that purchase, I feel better now.

We resume our nightly walks even though girls object. Andromeda towers over them and says, "It is non-negotiable, now put on that clothing Jules bought for you."

"But mother, we could cover that 7.5km walking track in an Earthian minute. We're bored walking with you; you are like, like, like so so slow and boring."

"I will race you, my daughters, if you want, but I would have to carry Jules on my back. He is only human, so you would all have an unfair advantage."

"OK mother, we will walk," they reply in unison. "But can we take our smartphones with us?"

"No, you cannot; this is going to be quality family time. We will do something called *talking* as well as walking."

The girls have a distinct look of displeasure, and one of them puts up the two-finger *V* on four of her hands a sign of defiance on Earth, when Andromeda is not looking, but they eventually comply. While walking back home, we pass that Muslim pastor again, who comments, "My, my, my, you have been very reproductive. Are you sure you don't want to join the local branch? We have relaxed the rules; praying is only required four times a day from now on."

For a moment, I consider his offer as I'm doing a lot of praying, then Andromeda interrupts my thoughts, "Thank you, sir, we shall consider your offer." Andromeda and I wave him goodbye.

"Andromeda, we have to think of some Earthly names for the girls. So far, we've called them Horsey01 to Horsey03 when they competed in those horse races. We have to get imaginative and think of some proper names."

"Jules, they do have real names, but they are not pronounceable on this planet. Their real names are high-frequency squeaks way above 20 kilohertz and not discernible to human hearing."

"Andromeda, if they stay here, they've got to get human-like names. How about Electronica, Neutronia and Protonia?"

"Jules, you are naming them after sub-atomic particles, but what about a last name? Our last name is based on a 16824 binary digit code followed by the first name. We can work that out later."

"I will propose the names to them. Now, Jules, can you keep the walking pace up, or I will have to drag you by your neck?"

"I'm doing my best, I only have two legs."

We get home, the girls are arguing. One of them says, "I do not want to be called Neutronia, and sis does not want to be called Protonia. They are not fundamental particles."

I look at them sternly. "What, would you want to be named? Up or Down Quarks, which are fundamental particles that make up protons and neutrons, or do you prefer we name you HiggsBogan, 1, 2, and 3? Make up your minds."

The girls look at one another, slightly stunned and chat. It's the first time I took a stern hand, and I'm looking really mean and annoyed.

"OK, we will accept the name change," they reply in unison. "We just have to decide who's going to be called Electronica as electrons are much smaller than protons or neutrons. Do you possess a weighing scale so that we can determine who shall be which?"

"I want to be Neutronia as neutrons consist of a positively charged proton and a negatively charged electron, and their relationship seems to work. They should swallow each other up, but they do not."

"Girls, that's like most human couples on Earth."

Andromeda comes over to me. "Let them argue Jules. The *Star Trek* episode is soon to start."

Andromeda and I lie on the floor, with pillows to rest our heads, and I turn on the TV and the volume is really up loud so we don't hear the girl octopi arguing. I wrap an arm around her.

"Jules, it is only going to get worse, well at least till they are equivalent to 27 Earth years old. They have to find boyfriends. Let us take them to the coast so they can do some deep-sea fishing. And yes Jules, if they are successful you will have to keep the pool spotless and order more seafood."

"Can't you just try ringing your mother again on the hyperphone? She must have the hyperdrive going again and can take them back to Authentica."

"Jules, I told you before that there are no male species left on our planet. Once they reproduce the male Octopi species will be taken to Authentica and genetically enhanced to be like us. I think I told you that a law has been passed on our planet that states that males cannot be eaten after copulation so we may be able to build up their population."

Star Trek starts on TV and we're furiously chewing popcorn. The kids come up from the basement and join us. They are watching intensely. The popcorn is soon consumed.

Luckily, I find six packets of salt and vinegar chips in the pantry else I could be part of the menu.

"Mum, their spaceship travels as fast as grandma's hyperdrive. Is it real?"

"Darling, they call it a warped drive and it will not be real for many centuries in this part of the galaxy."

Another daughter comments, "Those aliens, not the humans, on this TV show are really attractive. Can we watch more?"

"Darling, there is another episode to go. They have two of them on weeknights available for viewing."

"Mum, all those food TV advertisements are making us hungry. And what is funeral insurance? Those TV advertisements appear all the time."

"Darling, it helps remaining relatives to pay for their dead to be buried, incarcerated or incinerated."

"Mum, why do they not just recycle the dead; eat them like we do on our planet?"

"Shoosh, *Star Trek Voyager* is starting on TV."

And so once it's dark and we have watched the TV program, everyone except me dons their costumes. No, I'm not naked, I have shorts and a T-shirt on. We do our nightly walk, though the girls are impatient and sprint ahead to do the 7.5km river loop walk. They join us back 25.5 seconds later.

"Andromeda, they're slowing down."

"Jules, stop buying that junk food you have in your pantry. It is affecting them, and they have put on a lot of weight."

We all go to our beds, and so another night ends and all is well considering the circumstances. "Andromeda, are you fantasising about those aliens on that *Star Trek* TV show?"

"No Jules, most of those alien species depicted were former husbands of mine who got digested."

It's one of those moments when you feel like chewing your arm off, but I only got two, so I chew on the pillow instead till some logic returns. Eventually, I put my arms around the sleeping Andromeda and join her in her dreams.

CHAPTER 13

I get a phone call, "Jules, I have returned back to my planet but just for a brief visit. I'll only be gone for four hours in Earth time though weeks in our time."

"Andromeda, can you leave me that hyperspace cell phone device call-back number details because it just pops up as these mixed-up characters on my phone screen?"

"Why, Jules, I will return in a very short Earthian time? You don't need it."

I vigorously rub my head and try to regain some rational thinking and reply. "This high oxygen level and high gravity on Earth is not doing you or the kids any good. You're prematurely ageing, but I'll ring several times a day. I'll work out how to use that number."

That was definitely not a diplomatic comment on my part, and I rub my two black eyes after she returns. I look at the three Authentican girls. They haven't grown at all since moving to Earth. They're half the size of their mother. Earth is not their planet and they're ageing fast as well. They have to get back home, and so does Andromeda, if they want to live.

I dial my mother-in-law on the hyperphone. "Can you come over and take them back to *Authentica*? Long-term stays on Earth are not doing them any good. Maybe take them to that planet called Mars. Apparently, that Leo Musket guy is planning an expedition there soon. It's very low in oxygen, and the gravity is lower than Earth's, so it would resemble your planet, *Authentica* and keep your longevity intact."

"All right, I'll come over, but have their bags packed, and we will not go to Mars, but back to our planet, and I respect you for your concern," my octopus-like mother-in-law says.

"It's because I love you, even if you're far away, but I don't want to attend your funerals if you stay on Earth. Go now," I plead to Andromeda and the girls. I give Andromeda a huge kiss, close my eyes and hug the stepdaughters before they enter the hyperdrive device. I also hand a big box full of my *Star Trek* DVDs to Andromeda. She is thrilled.

"Jules, you remind me of that handsome *Captain Kirk* character in the first series of *Star Trek*." Then she giggles. "*Just joking*, as they say on your Earthian planet."

I'm not sure if I accept that as a compliment. Andromeda looks back. "Jules, I will be monitoring your Internet traffic. You better not join the *AlienSingles* dating site again or any other site. You could come for a brief visit to Authentica if you wear oxygen tanks. Mum can fire up the hyperdrive again and bring you over."

"I won't look at that alien dating site or even use my imagination, I promise." I throw her a kiss and she reciprocates.

In the deep throes of depression, I try to keep busy screwing and drilling, repairperson type of work, trying to fix the house up and to keep my mind from thinking about Andromeda. Three weeks passed before she called me, even though I called her several times each Earth Day.

The voice is crackly. "Jules, I have over 200 missed calls from you. We have just adopted a new Internet and phone service technology called TokTakSok. It is what you call a bit *flaky*, not the fish kind, but it is getting better. I miss you so much."

"I miss you so much, too. How are my stepdaughters doing?"

"Jules, they are flourishing and now taller and bigger than me in mass. They are attending the equivalent of what you call university. They are studying *ExtraTerrestrialLifeForms* and they have plenty of experience and can contribute to discussions. Their graduation ceremony will be in 100 Earth years' time. I hope you can attend."

"Can you transport my ashes over for the ceremony?"

"Sorry Jules, I forgot you humans have such a limited life span. I almost forgot to say that they love their new names. They are a hit with the boys, and now all the other girls on Authentica are changing their names, even the boys. Our scientists cannot keep up discovering more sub-atomic particles, so they just make them up just like they do on Earth."

"How about Neutrino? They're everywhere in the Universe. No, on second thought, that's a boy's name."

"Jules, the Neutrino is the smallest sub-atomic particle there is. No boy would want to be called that."

"Then, how about Photon or Photona, and has the male population recovered on your planet?" I ask.

"It is getting there, Jules, though not enough for our females to have multiple husbands just yet."

"Andromeda, how about you ask your mum if she can bring you to Earth in the hyperdrive, just for a few hours."

"Jules, Mum crashed the hyperdrive into one of our moons. She was stalking, sorry meant talking to a young Authentican boy at the time, and probably a bit hungry. A rescue team brought her back. She is now doing the equivalent of 500 Earth years of community service."

"Are there other hyperdrives you can purchase and drive?"

"Jules, the hyperdrive was unique, developed by one of my dads, I cannot remember which one, but he did not document the technology. He was what you would call on your planet a *mad scientist*."

After two more Earth months pass, I still speak to Andromeda for many hours every day on the hyperphone. Sure, we argue sometimes, but overall, life is good. I hope she comes back soon, as my typing fingers are starting to get itchy to go back to that AlienDating site.

"Andromeda, when I'm incinerated, I hope you remarry now that the male population on your planet has recovered in numbers."

"Jules, I would stay a window, sorry meant widow. I got used to your weirdness, which no one on our planet could ever match. You set a new low standard, sorry meant high standard."

I get photos and videos almost every day on the hyper Internet. I think the stepdaughters are smiling. They all point the two fingers with all eight arms before they burst out in laughter. I point my two fingers back on only two hands. They giggle again.

"Girls, I'd send you a present for your birthdays if your grandmother's hyperdrive was working."

"Stepdad, Authentica orbits our sun every 57 seconds, so better have many birthday presents. We're 300,000 years old, so you better have plenty of birthday presents ready."

Suddenly the radio channel I usually listen to changes to another as if by remote control, not by me. A song starts playing *Righteous Brothers – Unchained Melody*. I listen to it at least 100 times and have many buckets of tears waiting to be emptied.

I ring Andromeda on the hyperphone, "I hope you all come back soon. I miss you all so much."

"We will be on the way soon, maybe in an Earth week's time, but there is a malfunction in the new, latest design hyperdrive, and I am just attempting to fix it. Did you like the song?"

CHAPTER 14

I'm still feeling depressed thinking about and missing Andromeda. I drive back to Byron Bay to get some more of those magic mushies, which contain a mind-altering substance called Psilocybin. In small doses, it can be helpful in depression disorders; well, at least that's what I read. That's where I met her. We bumped heads while crawling on the ground and picking magic muchies. Some of the flowers in her hair fell out, flowers everywhere as she shook and rubbed her head. She looks like one of those hippies in the late 1960's but a lot worse for wear.

"My name is Golden Princess," she says.

"Mine is Jules, can I just call you GP?" I reply. I resist telling her that maybe she should change her name to Silver Princess, as her hair is somewhat white and she's quite dishevelled and very wrinkly.

"Yes, you can call me GP, but I don't have a medical degree. Do you want to come back to my place? It's only a shack just over that hill."

"I'm married," I reply.

"I'm not after you honey, or your money, but who is she?"

"She's an Octopus-like person from the planet Authentica."

"Darl, you better not take any more of those munchies again, else you'll end up in a psyche ward if you live anywhere else but Byron Bay, but you'd be fine in this town as we're all off the planet. Here's my phone number and address if you want some company and somewhere to stay."

I stay in the forest and munch on a few more of those bitter mushrooms, then wander into town. I'm hallucinating; Octopi everywhere, and I'm trying to hug them all. Unfortunately, one is the local police officer, but he's probably used to that stuff at Byron Bay, arrests me and takes me into custody. I spend the night in comfortable jail, and I'm allowed to leave the next day after a couple of cups of coffee.

I finally find my car and drive to GP's place.

"You mind if I stay the night? I spent last night in jail and didn't get any sleep due to all the noise from all these people wandering around their prison cells and hallucinating in wonder. I don't think I'd better drive back to Brisbane tonight."

"There's the couch, honey."

GP's shack is definitely not 5-star accommodation; more plant leaves inside than outside in the garden. I don't think it has ever been vacuumed. She points me to the couch. I look around. There are crosses, religious pictures, and rosary beads hanging on the walls and insects and spiders climbing amongst the hangings. It seems incongruous, but that's something we humans are good at – not making any logical sense.

I fall asleep almost instantly and don't have any dreams that I can remember. When I wake up the next morning, I see little fleas jumping all over me and getting a blood feast. I call out to GP, "Have you got any insect spray? I'm getting eaten alive!"

GP has this old record player that plays vinyl records. A song is playing, or more accurately, crackling – it's by a singer from the 1960s called Burl Ives, and the song is called "*Royal Telephone.*"

"GP, God did not protect me from fleas."

"Jules, we co-exist with bugs in this town, and we are Avonists. We don't use pesticides, only makeup which protects our skin from anything that needs protecting."

"GP, I'm heading home. I have a phone call to make. Could I have a strong coffee?" I ask as frantically scratching the itches from fleabites. I skol the coffee, which luckily is not hot; in fact, it's cold. I look down at the empty cup. There are little worms slithering around, so much for hygiene standards. I just hope I can make the two-hour drive back before my gut explodes and I soil the car seat.

"Do you want anything stronger? There are plenty of others I got." She asks. "You can use my phone if it's urgent," GP says.

"Thanks, but I have to use my royal telephone, which is back in Brisbane.

I run out to the car and bring back the bag of munchies I had previously collected.

"GP, thanks, you can keep these. I think I'll stay off them for a while. Thanks for letting me stay."

I rush to the car. I got a hyperspace phone call to make. I arrive home. There are six missed phone calls on the hyperphone. I quickly dial. She answers.

"Where have you been? I have been trying to call you for the last 2 Earth days. You better not be playing up."

"Believe me, the only thing that entered my mouth was some mushrooms. No other parts of the body were ever used, except for my hands, and that was only to scratch flea bites."

"Jules, we have towed back my mother's hyperdrive with my mother included. She is still breathing. She had another minor accident and is doing community service work. How about I make a visit, but for two days only? Now Jules, I took that CD you had and played it. It was by a person called *Sophie B. Hawkins*, and the song is called *As I Lay Me Down*. Listen on the hyperphone, I am putting it on."

I do. I listen to the song. Tears form in my eyes.

"Of course, I'd be overjoyed if you'd drop in, and I will wake up happy. By the way, can you still run and win a horse race like my stepdaughters did? The Melbourne Cup race is in two weeks' time."

I continue raving, "The phone bills for interstellar communication are horrendous on this planet, and I'm getting down to the poverty line trying to pay for them. You have to run."

"Jules, just sell the rest of my wedding rings, and are they still fighting on your planet?"

"More fighting and wars than ever," I reply. "I can now fully understand why you initially got rid of all the males on your planet. Maybe you can send our daughters down as well. Maybe they can make a meal of these warring leaders on Earth."

"Jules, I'm just reading the 2-page manual on how to use the reconditioned hyperdrive. It is written in very small print, but I got my four-eye seeing glasses, so I am nearly there. You had better drive down to that guy Harry, whom you know. I am very hungry, so order plenty of squid."

For a moment, the thought crosses my mind that there might be a correlation between how many arms you've got and how many eyes. It's certainly cheaper having only two eyes when you have to go to the optometrist.

"How are my stepdaughters doing?"

"I will tell you when I land at your home. It will not take long."

I await her arrival. Tears are forming in my eyes. I stop scratching the flea bites and pick up the Earth phone. "Harry, could I have 100kg of squid delivered?"

"Do you want them alive or dead?"

"Probably dead and ready for eating."

PS1: No substances of any illegal kind were taken, and this chapter is not an endorsement for taking drugs, natural or synthetic, to reduce the pain of loss. I was just totally intoxicated on alcohol, a legal drug, when I wrote this story, totally legal.

PS2: There is some scientific evidence that controlled administration of Psilocybin (a psychogenic substance found in magic mushrooms) can reduce the symptoms of depression, but only in very small doses. It needs more investigation, though the Pharmo companies won't like it. There are clinical studies happening in some European countries at the moment. Google it if you want to know more.

PS3: Another song to listen to on YouTube if you're into the sixties, *Where Have All the Flowers Gone*. It's an old anti-war song. Thanks, GP, for emailing it to me. I luv it.

CHAPTER 15

There's a flash of light in my lounge room as the hyperdrive refrigerator-like device materialises. Out steps Andromeda holding lots of baggage. I rush over to her and give her a hug.

"Jules, can you help me set up these devices? One is an anti-gravitron. It will lower the force of gravity within 50 metres of your house. You may feel a bit floaty and do not trust the bathroom weight scale as it will be fooled, and you might think that you do not have to control your calorie intake." I desist from saying that I felt more than a little bit floaty a few days ago after those magic munchies.

"Jules, this is the hypobaric chamber. It provides a low-pressure oxygen environment. We have to assemble it. I cannot sleep in the same room as you do, and you cannot sleep in this chamber unless you can hold your breath for 8 hours or more."

This is definitely not going to be a romantic night.

"Andromeda, how come the daughters did so well, winning the Melbourne Cup twice?"

"Jules, they had more than 500% oxygen level in their blood that they were not used to on Authentica, so of course they could run very fast. Now I can hardly persuade them to move or get out of bed. An Earthian snail could beat them in a race."

"Andromeda, you don't have to live to the equivalent of 50,000 Earth years. If you stay here on Earth without this equipment, we'll all pass away at roughly the same time as me, and whoever departs last takes this little cyanide pill; we'll die together."

"Jules, that is so romantic, but what if I just pretend I am dead?"

I don't answer.

"Andromeda, look, I purchased a lot of skin conditioner. It's natural and pesticide-free. Try it."

It's definitely not a good idea for a male to buy female skin conditioner products or mouth sanitisers, but only perfume or flowers. However, you learn these things the hard way.

"Andromeda, what if the girls come back here to Earth? There should be no more horsey racing, just study so they could finish their university degree in three years, instead of 100 years, and then they can go on to perhaps further study. Their lifespan would end up matching Earthians."

"Jules, they may be discriminated against if living here on this planet."

"Discrimination, that's part of life living on this planet; you get used to it, providing your skin colour is white," I reply. Then I look out from my balcony to the backyard next door; all these highly tanned young people, sipping champagne and lying on towels by their pool and absorbing the sun's ultraviolet rays. It seems to me they're trying to make a political statement and want to be black so as to protest against discrimination.

"Am I a beneficiary in your Will, not that you possess much?" Andromeda asks.

"No, I've been slack, I haven't made a death Will, plus I haven't got much as you said. Now, Andromeda, let's give it a try; call my stepdaughters and tell them no more horse racing if they come to Earth."

We ring on the hyperphone. Neutronia answers.

"Mum, are you OK? You haven't eaten Stepdad, I hope, not just because you could absorb a lot of toxic earthly substances, like those heavy metals found in earthly food. And mum Protonia, Electronica and I have developed an only slightly invasive device that humans can use to suck out the heavy metals so they can lose weight without any dieting."

"Enough speculation, dears. Jules is still breathing unassisted, and he does not weigh that much or is attracted to magnets. Now girls, I am going to ask you if you want to come back to earth. The University degrees here take 3 years, not 100, and Jules has promised we would move close to the ocean, so there are plenty of Octopi guys you could meet up with unless you become caught in fishing nets."

"Mum, I shall discuss it with my sisters, but what is the downside?"

"Darling, you will not live 50,000,000 years. Here on Earth, you may make it to 80 or 100 Earth years of age, but you will not be bored on this planet. There is so much going on. You could start writing ridiculous satire books like Jules does."

"Mum, have you still got my favourite teddy bear? Sorry, I meant the vibrating battery-powered octopus bear."

"Darling, Jules has kept all your toys, some of which I do not approve of, but they are still all here."

"And mum, can we run in that horse race again, just once more, the Melbourne Cup one? It was fun."

"Darlings, you will have to crawl out of bed and do some training. The carbon dioxide levels are increasing here on Earth, so you may not be as fast as before."

"Sounds good, Mum, we love carbon dioxide. It means we do not have to eat as much of that boring squid, though squid is better than eating humans. Oops, I did not mean that last comment. Delete it. Sis's are packing now, but we got a Godwormiglow as a pet; it is a bit like a dog. Can he come too?"

"Jules, is that OK?"

"It's OK, we have a big garden."

"Stepdad, the Godwormiglow, who we call Trumpy, does not like the outdoors except for golf courses. He is a bit primitive and has some weird ideas, but you do not have to listen to him. Just give him a pat on that horrible haircut he has on his head."

"No problem, you can bring Trumpy the Godwormiglow as well."

"I'm sending the hyperdrive back, but read the instructions as some of the controls have changed," Andromeda says. "It has been programmed to return here to Earth."

Andromeda wacks that glass of wine from my hand. I guess I'll have to find more creative spirits.

I wrap my two arms around her, and we continue watching the *Star Trek* episodes. Then there's a blinding flash as the hyperdrive materializes in the kitchen. The girls slither out, and so does Trumpy. I give the girls a hug, but not Trumpy.

There's much fun as we reunite, and all the squids get furiously devoured by the girls with bits hanging from the corners of their mouths as they nod their heads to each other. Trumpy, who looks like a burly, furry dog and whose face resembles someone quite prominent in USA politics, brushes his hair whilst tweeting. I put him outside and lock him in the metal shed, something known as a Faraday cage, as any metal-enclosed storage is; no radio waves can get in or out, so tweeting is impossible. I shut the windows so we can't hear Trumpy whining and screaming.

Next day, I had to bury Trumpy. He passed away overnight, probably from lack of tweeting, because we certainly gave him plenty of squid and water, so it wasn't lack of eating. We all stood there, me pretending to be mourning, whilst we did the funeral-type burial thing. The girls are shedding tears from each of their four eyes.

"He was a good pet," one of the girls says, and then we all go inside the house.

I wrap my two arms around Andromeda again and wonder what may come next.

CHAPTER 16

The Covid-19 restrictions have been relaxed, so the five of us can get back to doing a nightly walk. Andromeda measures the girls, and I order online three more of those long gowns called Burqas, much bigger in length and girth than the previous ones they had. An email arrives from the distributor.

"Sir, your daughters have grown very quickly since your last purchase. We do not have any in stock for their height, but I am sure I can have some quickly made. It might take a day or two. We also now encourage girls to play basketball or Netball. You should get your daughters to join a club or join ours, the *ABC*, short for *Allah Basketball Club*."

I reply, "Thank you, sir. We shall consider your offer, though at the moment, they want to pursue a running career."

Being polite always helps. The delivery of the gowns happens next day. That night, we go walking along the river, covered head to feet in clothing and veils. I can feel the tension. The girls just want to jump into the river to cool off, but I explain to them that there are Bull sharks in the Brisbane

River, and those sharks are very big and mean and like eating humans, which is a delicacy to them.

"Yum, yum," they say in unison. I guess the Bull sharks wouldn't stand a chance, and it could cut down on food bills as well as save the wider Brisbane community if they venture into the river. It would be a win-win. I'll discuss that with Andromeda later.

"Darlings, let us just keep walking. Jules is refilling the swimming pool so you can go swimming again."

While walking, we encounter that preacher guy again. "My, my, how your daughters have grown in six months. Are you sure you don't wish to join our prayer sessions? We have them in the park these days."

Andromeda diplomatically replies, "Thank you, sir; we shall consider your offer, but believe me, we are praying very much or at least my husband is."

After the walk, I ring Harry. "Jules, I haven't heard from you for over 6 months. How are things?"

"Harry, it's complicated, but can we resume the 100kg daily orders of seafood again?"

"Yeh, sure Jules."

"Oh, one other thing, Harry, can you source three live giant male Octopi and deliver them to my salt-water swimming pool?"

"Jules, I told you before I can't tell the difference."

"I'll get one of my daughters online. She'll describe the intricacies: Harry, it's all in the name of science; my daughters are doing degrees in Macrobiology, and they need some living male Octopi specimens to study."

"I can do that, and you should apply to be a contestant on that reality TV show called *OZ Most Weirdest*; you'd win for certain."

"Thanks, Harry, I'll certainly consider it."

"How are you going to pay?"

"Another one of those gold rings, Harry. It should cover the costs for the next 6 months."

"Jules, I gave the last one to my wife. She wears it on her wrist. She has very big wrists."

"Harry, just melt the next one down. You'll get at least 20 finger rings out of that huge one, and you'll keep your wife happy."

"Jules, I'm not a psychologist, but I detect some cynicism. Is everything OK?"

"Harry, one day I'll explain it all."

I go back to Andromeda and wonder how this extraterrestrial relationship can survive. Andromeda has that uncanny ability to read people's faces, not their thoughts, well probably their thoughts as well, unless you are a psychopath, and you have no facial expressions like a poker face. She moves towards me and wraps her eight arms around me. "Do not worry; it will be alright, as humans do not taste that good."

She seductively hands me an apple, "Eat this fruit, Jules. You need some vitamin C. It is from Authentica and grown in a hydroponic garden." She must have read our Earthian religious myths, the *Adam and Eve* story. I take the bite. Oh gawd, that one apple bite is more powerful than twenty magic munchies. I'm definitely going to be banished to hell, which is fine, as they definitely have more fun in hell than in heaven.

Two hours pass in vivid imaginations – I'm Adam, and Andromeda is a sort of Eve with only two arms and two legs. A few unmentionable interactions happen.

"Andromeda, can we grow these magic apples here on Earth?"

"Jules, we could, but I do not think your alcohol industry would approve as it would be competition, and they have a big influence and control over your governments."

I can just imagine an 18+-year-old ordering an apple when they go to a rave concert or a music pub. It won't work. It's not cool. Well, not yet.

CHAPTER 17

"Andromeda, can't we use the hyperdrive to get to Melbourne for the Cup race?"

"Jules, the hyperdrive would not survive the load as I have not yet properly fixed the payload shrinking device. We have to shrink to fit into the hyperdrive and then expand once we complete the journey. Phone that Harry guy, he may lend you a truck for us to travel in."

I ring Harry. "Harry, can I borrow one of your big vans again? My wife and my very big stepdaughters would like to make a trip to Melbourne, and they all won't fit in my two-seater car."

"Yes, sure Jules. You are my best customer, but why don't you just catch an aeroplane?"

"Harry, each of my daughters would occupy at least three plane seats and my wife 2. Nine seats in total would have to be purchased. It's economically unfeasible."

"Jules, I've sourced a new supply of squid called *Diet Lite Squid*, which you may order next time instead of the regular. They may lose some weight."

"Good idea, Harry. It's always diet light squid when I next make an order, but now, can I come over to pick up the van?"

"Sure, Jules."

"Andromeda, did you enlarge those horse outfits?"

"Jules, I am still sewing."

I call the girls and they come out of the pool.

"Girls, you've got to qualify again for the race, but don't run faster than 3 minutes, or the authorities will suspect that something is dodgy or Octopussy."

"Electronica replies, "I thought they would pick that up earlier by looking at those comical horse costumes we have to wear to compete in the last race. Those costumes will slow us down."

"OK, you understand, not to do more than 3 minutes, sorry meant less than 3 minutes for the qualifying trials, and when you race in the Cup, you come first, second and third, but you only win by a head away from the other horses."

"Stepdad, we could run that course in less than one minute despite these ridiculous costumes on."

"Electronica, you've got to think about the welfare of real horses. They'd become depressed and never race again if the margin is unachievable. They'd end up in the meatworks."

"Stepdad, you're chewing on a burger at the moment. How do you know it's not a horsey burger?"

"Electronica, it's not. We send most of our retired racehorses to meatworks overseas. You better watch out."

The girls are arguing. "It's my turn to come first."

We find a disused warehouse in the Melbourne suburb called Flemington. It's not luxury, but it's close to the racetrack. We're all tired after the 16-hour drive, but luckily there's a Fish&Chips shop nearby.

Next day, the girls all qualify, and after the Melbourne Cup race, they were awarded first, second and third again. They are on the podium, making horse-grunting noises. The cup presentation ceremony was a bit unusual and made many mouths gape and possibly dislocate. Some patrons fainted. Luckily, there were plenty of ambulance officers present when the girls took off their costumes, which wasn't part of the original plan, and caused traffic chaos as some terror-stricken racegoers rushed away and didn't check for traffic in the streets.

CHAPTER 18

Those intoxicated, who are most people at a horse race, were aghast, but some thought it was all a joke and part of the after-Melbourne Cup entertainment, and so started clapping and laughing.

Protonia grabs the microphone from the host. "We have learnt English from watching that *My Kitchen Rules*, Earthian TV show. Our home is 40 light years away, but we have devices that can suck up your TV transmissions and reduce their travel time."

The remaining audience laughs again. They must think it's a comedy act. Protonia continues her speech. "Your cultures on this planet discriminate against anyone or anything that is different. My stepfather's parents came from a different country on your planet, and they were called wogs and were looked down upon."

She raises only two arms and yells, "Discrimination must stop!"

Some of the audience clap and cheer whilst others still appear very confused and wave their heads from side to side.

Protonia continues her speech. "My two sisters and I will be starting a new political party. It will be called em, em, *The Wog Party*, yes, *The Wog Party*. Please vote for us if you believe in equality, justice, and not based on any religious beliefs or ethnicity or how many limbs you possess."

Someone from the audience yells out, "What if we don't vote for you?"

Protonia replies, "Well, I guess we will just have to eat you."

The audience laughs. They didn't know that Protonia was absolutely deadly serious.

The three Octopi girls moved to separate apartments in the northern suburbs of Melbourne, in different electorates, ones full of overseas born ethnic people and campaigned. Andromeda and I visit on average every second day when they all get together to discuss tactics. Andromeda makes the journey from Brisbane to Melbourne, with me on her back, in 35 minutes and 59 seconds. She is slowing down; it must be old age, but I'd never say that to her.

Sometimes the girls are very busy, each typing simultaneously on many laptop computers, whilst answering phone calls from constituents, so we don't have a chance to talk with them.

The three girls comfortably won their seats at the State elections after a vigorous campaign that included many TV interviews and doorknocking. They are making a positive change. They work as a collective, as they always have. I can't distinguish one from the other, so I make them wear name tags when we see each other, though sometimes they swap tags and have a laugh at my expense. They also bought an apartment for Andromeda and me to stay in when we are visiting. We seem to be spending more and more time in that apartment in Melbourne.

I ask Andromeda, "How can you distinguish which girl is which?"

"Jules, we have highly developed olfactory glands. Even though they look the same, each one smells slightly different. I identify them by their smell."

That comment got me worried. I'll have to install a high-performance exhaust fan in our toilet and also shower more frequently.

The girls run over to visit after a long day in parliament. They take off their sunglasses. They are very fancily dressed. We are sitting at the table having a vegetarian feast as they have become vegetarian. It took 100kg of veggies, 20kg of lentils, four dozen eggs, and many hours of cooking to feed them. I secretly wish they'd kept with the raw squid diet, which required no preparation.

"Mum, would you have done things differently if you had a second chance?" Neutronia asks.

"Neutronia, life is like a spider web. The spider can go in many directions. Just one little circumstance, like a slight breeze or an insect caught in the web, can shift the spider's direction for life."

We all put our arms around each other, though I'm a bit limited. "It's *Star Trek* TV time," I yell out. We all sit on the couch and bean bags in front of the TV and watch a recorded TV video.

"Stepdad, we've seen this episode before," Electronica calls out.

Well, there's one good thing about dementia; you can watch the same episodes over and over and they all seem like new.

"Electronica, just stay patient for the next 5 minutes. A new episode on live TV is about to start. Here, have some squid chips," I say.

"Stepdad, we are like on this vego journey thingo. We do not eat that stuff anymore, as most of the people who voted for us are left-wing vegetarians who wear designer clothing and drive fancy cars. Like, like, we cannot be seen as hypocrites, especially in public, you understand. By the way, do you like our new costumes? They were made by Buddhist Dior or was it Christian Dior, especially for us."

And I thought they only had millennials on Earth. I rush to the pantry and pull out five packets of salt and vinegar potato crisps. Yep, I emptied the supermarket shelves of crisps and hoarded them during the Covid-19++ epidemic; in fact, I have a garage full of them. I just wish I had hoarded more toilet paper for when the girls come over.

And so, the next *Star Trek* episode starts. Our eyes are all glued to the screen, and we're furiously munching potato crisps. The crisps don't satisfy me. I get a severe case of the munchies and get some of that defrosted squid. I don't want it going to waste, so I pour some vinegar and salt on the squid and start chewing. In my haste, I forgot to cook the squid, just chewed it raw.

"You're disgusting, stepdad. Move away from us. It is people like you who will cause an environmental crisis and the death of all sea creatures on this planet. Stop eating those squids. We will give them a dignified burial in your backyard. We will even sing at their funeral."

I whisper to Andromeda, "Do you want a chew?"

She whispers back, "Jules, Harry rang earlier. He said that the last batch of squid was infected with a pathogen that causes high-intensity stomach contractions and massive expulsions of semi-processed matter from the posterior an hour post-consumption."

Luckily, the stepkids didn't hear that conversation.

Mum, "That *Captain Janeway* character on that *Star Trek Voyager* series is really cool. Is cool the right term to use on this planet? We do not want to freeze."

There's a commercial on TV, a brief break. "Jules, grab some more of those crisps from the kitchen. The girls chew loudly, so turn the TV volume up louder," Andromeda whispers.

"I can't, Andromeda, I've got to make a rush for the loo, my stomach is severely rumbling and about to explode. You know where the crisps are kept and turn the volume on the TV up really loud."

I should have shut the bathroom window. My sensitive neighbours called the police because they thought the explosive sounds from my bathroom were due to a terrorist attack. A squad of police cars, sirens blurring, arrive. The doorbell rings. I answer and walk out with my pants half down. The police officers are heavily armed and glance side-to-side, ready to shoot. One of them calls out, "What's that horrible smell? Is it an explosive device? It's not an incendiary substance. Incendiary substances don't smell that bad. Sir, you better have a long, long shower and keep the bathroom window shut," the police sergeant says with a smile and then leaves. I can hear them hysterically laughing at my expense as they hop into their police cars.

Andromeda comes over to me. "Jules, it's OK, though I will not be giving you a kiss at the moment. Now, can you pull your pants up and turn the exhaust fan on in the bathroom?"

I oblige and do as she beckons. She's always a woman to me and always has to be right.

CHAPTER 19

"Mum, we have to leave; we have a busy day tomorrow in Parliament."

"Jules, can you call a taxi for the girls?" Andromeda asks.

"Mum and Jules, it is OK. We can sprint to our apartments in under 10 seconds, provided we get green traffic lights."

Andromeda intercedes, "Girls, it is dangerous for females to be out at this late time of the night. What if you get only red traffic lights?"

Neutronia replies, "Mum, we can handle that."

"No, you cannot, you have become a vego. You cannot eat any human assailants anymore."

"Mum, we might make exceptions."

Andromeda says no, "Jules will drive you in that van that Harry gave to us because it smells so much of squid. Harry should have given that vehicle to you. You made him rich with all the squid purchases, and I've been informed that he is basking on lounges in the Bahamas, with sunglasses on, surrounded by Earthling females, not squid females."

I press the ignition key. Harry's van battery is flat.

One of the girls offers to give a push start to the van. Accepting the offer was almost a fatal mistake as I dodge trees and street signs, but eventually gain control of the van and the motor starts. I drive them back to their abodes.

"Stepdad, will you stay with Mum? It's not like you are capable of conducting any reproductive activities?"

"Electronica, Neutronica or Protonica, whichever one you are, we don't do those things at our age, though we do fiddle a bit with each other whilst watching *Star Trek* when you're not around. We love each other's company very much, so we are very likely to stay together."

I lied, but I've learnt to hold my breath for 5 minutes. Tongue kissing with an Authentecian species, with a very long tongue, is a definitely challenging experience whilst your face turns a brighter shade of pale and you try not to choke. You really have to hyperventilate a lot before indulging in the experience.

"Andromeda, the girls are working very hard and, against all odds, have introduced many species, gender and environmental reforms in our Parliament. Perhaps they should go on holiday back to Authentica and have some fun. I'm sure the male species has regenerated by now."

"Jules, I will check if the hyperdrive is still working, but they did whisper to me whilst you were getting crisps, that they have plenty of human males trying to court them. They seem happy and occupied on Earth. It worked for you and me, so it can work for them. Have you got any more *Star Trek* episodes?"

"Andromeda, we've seen all the *Star Trek* series in my DVD collection, but I've got some of the Alien movies with that actress called *Sigourney Weaver*. That alien creature in the movie may be a very distant relative of yours. It's got many legs."

It was definitely very politically incorrect to even suggest that the monstrous creature in the *Alien* movie could somehow have a resemblance to Andromeda, even though they do have a similar number of arms or legs. There are eight hands shaking my throat, and it's hard to type in this situation without making a lot of typos.

"Andromeda let go; it was just a joke. You are a trillion times more attractive than that creature in the movie."

She releases her grip, and I gasp for air. I have to get rid of those *Alien* Movie DVDs and only keep the movies where the alien females are attractive. I guess that's why she likes the *Star Trek* TV series.

"What other movies have you got?" She asks.

"Look in my DVD storage cabinet, there are over 200 there."

"Jules, there's a movie called *Romeo and Juliet*. Let us put it on, and if there are any crisps left, can you get some packets?"

And so, we lie on the bean bags next to each other, watching the movie and chewing salt and vinegar potato crisps.

The movie finishes.

"Jules, do they really do things on this planet that way?"

"Some do and succeed, but now there are a lot of domestic violence issues here, often related to drug use. Hopefully, the girls can fix that."

"I hope they do too. Now, Jules, have you got any other good movies?"

"Andromeda, how about we watch this series. It's called *Miss Fisher's Murder Mysteries*.

"Turn it on Jules." I do.

She whispers, "Do you think I look slightly like that actress who plays Miss Fisher, even though she has only two arms and two legs?"

After these many years together, I've learnt that a little bit of diplomacy goes a long way and ensures one stays alive. "No comparison, you are a zillion times more beautiful."

She hugs me with all eight arms, which does make it hard to see the TV screen. I start hyperventilating, just as a precaution.

CHAPTER 20

"Andromeda, it's Friday night, and we have to cook. The girls and their Earthling partners will be here soon and probably ravenous."

"Jules, it is OK, relax. They said they would bring the food for this occasion, and they are driving over, not running over. They are trying not to over-impress their Earthian partners."

"I hope they have a big van," I say.

"Jules, the Earthians don't eat as much as we do. Our species do not have gut bacteria, so a lot of what we eat ends up undigested, well it ends up in what you call the toilet, but the water life is happy; plenty of nutrients in the bay and oceans, when the sewerage is released for the fish and squid to feed on."

The doorbell rings. Six beings wander in, including three humans, holding steaming pots of what smells like spicy vegetarian food and a big trolley with even more steaming food. I open the windows and turn the ceiling fans on to let the steam out, as I don't want to be scrubbing mould from the ceilings.

Andromeda announces, "This is Tricycle, Protonia's partner."

"Mam, my name is actually Triambent, not Tricycle; my parents were hippies, too. It's OK."

Andromeda continues the introductions. "This is Newbert, Neutronia's current partner."

Newbert is nondescript on the outside and has a slightly worried look on his face, but he politely says *hi* to everyone while looking down at the floor.

"This is Amorphice, Electonica's girlfriend and partner. She is a human as far as I can tell."

Amorphice has long, free-flowing hair, which partially conceals her face despite her colourful headband. Her parents must definitely have been hippies, as were all the other parents of my stepdaughter's partners. Amorphice is rather attractive, though she has red-dyed beaded hair, a ring through her nostrils, and a very colourful sense of dress. My mind briefly wonders what their bed life is like.

Andromeda whispers to each of her daughters, "Eat very, very slowly, look up, and indulge in the conversation. Do not gobble or wobble."

"But mum, this tastes so good. It's almost as good as eating a human, but well, we are vegos now, so we do not do that anymore," she whispers with a cheeky smile.

The girls restrain their appetites, and it's a very cordial night. A lot of booze was consumed, and our guests look very dozy, rolling their eyes.

I whisper, "Andromeda, they can't drive back or run back. They'll have to stay here for the night."

"Jules, let us retrieve the sleeping bags. They look too sleepy to attempt any bedroom gymnastics."

Next day, there are eight in all, humans and Authenticans, at the breakfast table; some worse for wear and rubbing their eyes.

"Mum, could I have a glass of squid juice?"

"Neutronica, I think you meant Sequoia juice, the tree juice."

"Yes, of course, that is what I meant, Mum."

One of the girls asks, "Stepdad, is the swimming pool clean?"

"It has a lot of algae floating in it," I reply.

"Yum, algae is vegetarian."

And so they all jump in the pool and splash water over each other as they frolic. The electric clothes dryer is going to be very busy tonight, as they don't strip down before jumping into the water. Andromeda wraps an arm around me. "Jules, shall we join them? We are not too old to have some fun."

"I have no bathers."

"Just strip down and jump in naked. No one will be overwhelmed by your down-under appendage."

Triambent, one of the human guys, jumps out of the pool and rushes to the van, and brings in a carton of champagne. He then rushes to the lounge room to bring out the wine glasses we were using. Unfortunately, he trips, and the wine glasses lie shattered. I jump out of the pool and sweep the broken glass into a corner, but don't bin them. I'm still rebelling against my pedantic father. What you can do tomorrow, do tomorrow, that's my motto.

I help Triambent stand up and carry the precious cargo to the pool. He is slightly bleeding. I find the band-aids, but a bit of blood seeps into the water. The girls have their tongues out. I hope it's just for the champagne. We swig from the bottles and pass them around.

"Andromeda, they can't drive back home again. We'll have to get the sleeping bags out again for another night."

We all lie on the floor with cushions in front of the TV set. I look in the video cabinet; there are definitely no more *Alien* movies.

"What about the *Rocky Horror Picture Show*? Says Neutrina.

I put the DVD on. I hope the neighbours can't hear because we're all doing the *Time Walk* dance: *A step to the left and a step to the right …'.*

Once the movie finished, it was certainly the most uncomfortable sleep you could ever have; on the lounge room floor without any pillows, still there are many arms wrapped around us.

Don't dream it, be it, reverberates in my mind.

I wake up at 4 am, start worrying, and rush to the pantry. What are we going to have for breakfast? I feel relieved; I'm glad the girls have become vegetarian, so I have nothing to fear.

"Stepdad, get the crisps out. We want to watch that movie again."

"You've got work tomorrow," I reply.

"Stepdad, we don't work that much in Parliament; it's mostly a non-cognitive show up, and we just try to join the other parliamentarians in dozing, but they snore so loudly and keep us awake; plus, this video is giving us ideas for our next speeches. We'll buy those electric cattle prods to keep those parliamentarians awake so they listen to our speeches."

I retrieve plenty of packets of crisps from the pantry, and we watch the same movie again and again, all huddled together, except for the dancing scenes when we all get up and dance again and again, and no one gets consumed except the potato crisps.

I whisper to Andromeda, "Do you think their relationship will last?"

"Jules, based on a sample size of three, it is probable one will," she says. It may not be a good idea to lecture Andromeda in statistics, at least not now.

Chapter 21

Andromeda does not seem well. She's splattering and coughing into a handkerchief.

"Andromeda, are you immune to this Corona Virus?"

"Jules, there are at least 3,700 coronaviruses on this planet transmitted by bats and monkeys, but most are harmless to humans. You probably have a few species living in your gut, but this is all new to my species, and I may have accidentally swallowed a bat when doing my morning run. We have little immunity to your viruses just yet, but our immune systems evolve very quickly."

"Andromeda, we'll keep socially isolated, well I mean you can still hug me, but we won't hug strangers."

"I am fine with that, Jules. Now, can you find my multi-phasic toothbrush?"

I'm super worried. I forget about the toothbrush. In my frenzy, I ring Protonia.

"Stepdad, our government Mental Health bill got approved. We all have to have our arms around each other and dance to that *Rocky Horror Time Warp* song for ten minutes every day, wearing face masks and maintaining a bit of social distance. The Left-wing, Right-wing, and Greenies have all collaborated for once. Those fat guys in Parliament will lose weight; it's a win-win. We're thrilled."

"Protonia, your mother is not well."

"What, what, what? I'm running over straight away."

"No Protonia, don't do that, at least not right now. I don't have any of those *N95* face masks. Stay at home. You can talk to her on the phone."

"Stepdad, you don't have a smartphone with a camera. I'm coming, so will my sisters."

I lay next to Andromeda as she struggles to breathe. The breathing ventilator I ordered has been delivered, and I read the instructions. The girls arrive more than a little bit sweaty after a 90-second run through peak-hour traffic. I wrap towels around what I think are their mouths and nasal cavities.

"Stay away; I'll insert the breathing ventilator tube."

"Stepdad, that's not her mouth. It's her behind!"

"OK, Protonia, you do the honours."

I lie next to Andromeda and embrace her as tears flow down my face. "Breathe on me, we'll die together."

Suddenly Andromeda springs up.

"Mum, you've recovered," the girls call out in joy.

"Darlings, I have, but Jules is struggling to breathe; we may have to drive him to a hospital; he is only human."

"Mum, can't we just stick that ventilator tube into one of his orifices?"

"No darling, it's hospital time. Here are the van keys. I'll sit with Jules in the back of the van."

One of the girls effortlessly lifts me and, not too gently, throws me into the back of the van. I may have acquired some very bruised ribs, which hurt more than the Coronavirus. At least when you feel pain, you know you're still alive. Andromeda is there at the hospital with me, in her long gown and veil. I'm struggling to breathe. "Jules, our race adapts quickly." She thrust her tongue into my mouth, and I get a huge dose of bad fish breath along with plenty of antibodies and oxygen. I recovered very quickly, though I'm not sure if it was the bad breath or antibodies that knocked out the virus;

more research needs to be done. Is the virus deterred by bad breath and then just hops to another host? There's a marketing opportunity if that is the case - Jules' *Anti-Viral Bad Breath Liquor Will Cause Any Virus To Move On And Find A More Palatable Host, So You'll Be Safe.*

"Andromeda, can we just get a taxi back home? I prefer that the girls don't drive us."

We're back home the next day. Andromeda is using all eight arms to massage my ribs. After a short while, the ribs don't hurt anymore. She's also brushing her teeth with the multi-phasic toothbrush. "Andromeda, we're out of toothpaste. What did you use?"

"Jules, I siphoned some petrol from the van. It kills most mouth-causing odour bacteria."

I'm glad we don't smoke cigarettes or use the gas oven; else the house would go up in flames. I open the windows to let the inflammable petrol fumes escape.

"Andromeda, I found some mouthwash in the bathroom; use all of it, and could you spend at least ten minutes swigging the stuff?"

She comes out of the bathroom, wobbling a little.

"Jules, that mouthwash tasted good, what is in it?" she says in a slightly slurring voice.

"It's alcohol, it kills almost anything."

She then slithers over to my video cabinet and pulls out a music CD.

"Jules, how about this one, *Fleetwood Mac,* and can you forward to the song *Sisters of the Moon*?

Stuff Coronavirus, Andromeda and I are madly gyrating in the lounge room with the stereo full blast. We repeat the song many, many times. Her breath and mine have settled down. We're very sweaty and spend 5 minutes in the shower afterwards.

I lay next to her, hug her, and whisper, "I'm the luckiest guy still alive."

She whispers back, "I am the luckiest Authentican alive, but do not count your blessings," she says, then gives a wink. She's definitely developing a wicked sense of humour, at least, I hope.

Chapter 22

The girls arrive again to check up on how we're doing.

"Mum, got anything to eat? We're like super hungry. We did the 20 km run in 50.5 seconds."

"Darlings, hop in the shower first, I'll see what Jules can do."

The girls oblige.

"Jules, what have we got?" Andromeda asks.

"Not too much in the freezer, but there are bananas and avocados ripening in the backyard."

Well, the girls did more damage than a possum plague could do. The avocado tree and banana plants are stripped of their fruit and leaves. I secretly wish they hadn't become vegetarian.

"What's for dessert, Mum?" Neutronia asks as she looks at me. On second thought, I'm glad they have become vegetarians.

"Darlings, we are fine. Now tell us what has been going on in your lives."

Electronica speaks up first. "Mum, we all got dumped by our Earthian partners; it's not good. We are like super, super, super depressed. I think we may stop eating and become anorexic and starve ourselves to death."

After witnessing my plants being devoured, I don't think that will ever happen.

"Come here, darlings, Jules, you join in too."

It is a breathtaking experience as 26 arms hug each other tightly. I gasp for air afterwards. I can feel their pain and my rib pain.

"Darlings, you are all to stay the night here; Jules will order breakfast. Heartbreak is part of life, especially when you are young."

"Mum, the three of us are so frustrated; they just keep bickering in Parliament over trivial things. They should replace all in parliament with those artificial intelligence (AI) devices. Some of those devices are far smarter than humans and even look like humans. The other day I was talking to this really nice Earthian guy, but then his head dropped and he whispered *I need a recharge, please help me to a charger*."

"Darlings, but who would make the decisions to program those devices and insert humanistic values into their so-called AI thinking? It could be greatly misused. Fortunately, we had no need for AI on Authentica as we used our own brains to great effect."

The girls flop down, making it difficult to walk around them without tripping over the kitchen table to get the potato crisps. I come over and give each one an individual hug, and then I get the mop to wipe away all our tears, about a bucket load, as they hug me.

"Girls, I love your mother and consequently I love you too and will take care of you."

"Stepdad, are you a sub-species called a paedophile?"

Luckily Andromeda intervened and set things straight. "Darlings, paedophiles are the lowest life forms on this planet. Jules is not one of them."

The girls relax, "Stepdad, what have you got that we can watch on the video device?"

"Protonia, check the video cabinet," Andromeda replies.

"What about this one? It's called *Smallville*, and it's about an outer-space guy, and stepdad has the whole collection. He must have liked the show."

"Put it on, darling," Andromeda says.

We're all lying on the bean bags and watching the whole first series.

"That *Clark Kent* guy is like a hunk, but we can run faster than him, though we haven't tried the flying bit just yet unless we purchase one of those capes."

Protonia says that she likes that *Lex Luthor* character, who is a very bad guy. That's certainly a worry.

A song comes on the radio: a *Tom Petty* song - *I'm Learning to Fly*. I try to imagine three large Octopi-like creatures flying. They'd need some very powerful anti-gravity devices, but then again, that may be just a song metaphor.

"Mum, that *Clark Kent* guy is like allergic to that green glowing stuff, and mum, why are people on this planet so entranced with the metal called gold?"

"Darling, our society used gold for the plumbing pipes back on Authentica. It is like the iron ore is on this planet, gold is everywhere on our planet and mostly treated as a waste product, but gold is rare on this planet darling, and humans like rare things."

For a moment, I wonder if she's subtly alluding to that's why I like her. She's definitely rare.

"Mum, were our ex-dads cheap skates? I mean, they could have bought iron rings that are rare on our planet, and Mum, why don't they just make engagement and wedding rings out of Uranium-235? It's rare as well."

"Darling, Uranium-235 is hard to obtain on Earth. Governments grab it all to make nuclear bombs, well they mine it, plus humans don't tolerate radiation as well as we do; their wedding ring fingers would rot and drop off."

I briefly imagine what a newly engaged couple, wearing their Uranium-235 rings, bring their hands close together for the kiss at the end of the ceremony. There would be a mushroom cloud rising above their suburb. OK, back to the here and now. I'll get Andromeda 8 rings made from iron or maybe the tops from aluminium cans, which are easier to get.

"Mum, we want to be superheroes, like that *Clark Kent*. We'll quit our jobs in parliament as parliament doesn't rescue people."

"Girls go to bed."

They slither downstairs to their makeshift bedroom, but an hour later both Andromeda and I can still hear very lively conversations coming from below. I briefly check on them from a corner. They appear to be hyperactive. I don't interfere, just go back upstairs.

"Andromeda, have you ever seen them behaving this way?"

"No Jules, but we'll get to the bottom of this in the morning. I am tired, let's just sleep."

"Andromeda, if they become superheroes, I could write some stories of their adventures. I'd call the stories 'NPE' after Neutronica, Protonica and Electronica. Marvel Comics better watch out."

"Jules, you may be more delusional than my daughters are at the moment. Now stop pacing around and come to bed."

Chapter 23

I wake up. Andromeda is sitting in front of my computer, Googling.

"Jules, avocados contain substances that may make our species highly delusional, a bit like the magic mushrooms that you once ingested. We have to discourage them from quitting their jobs. Write the comic story, but do not base it on real life."

For a moment, I think. My favourite fruit, avocado, will not be allowed in this household ever again. I'll have to purchase them at the fruit market and sit huddled up, with my hoody on, in a dark alleyway, while I squeeze lime juice, with a bit of potassium salt, onto the sliced, peeled halves of avocado and then gobble them up; yum.

"Jules, can you also hide those superhero DVD movies you own? They may be contributing to the girls' delusions."

"Andromeda, the girls ate those big pips inside the avocado as well. They ate the whole fruit, skin and pips. We have to do some scientific research; how about an experiment?"

The girls come down the stairs into the lounge room looking worse for wear. They flop on the couch instead of the beanbags.

"Darlings, you all have dark rings under all your eyes. Did you sleep at all?"

"No, Mum, we just had ridiculous conversations about how to save the planets, Authentica and Earth. I think we're now back to normal, but very tired."

"Darlings, don't go to work today, you need to rest."

"Mum, we have to go back to our Earthly homes. We got work to do."

Andromeda and I watch them leave as they sprint off, but Electronica bangs into an electricity pole and brings down the electricity powerlines in our suburb. There are sparking, short-circuiting wires everywhere, causing a major power failure in our neighbourhood.

Andromeda, I, and the other two girls come rushing over.

Andromeda asks, "Are you all right, my darling?"

"I am Mum, I've been recharged."

I look around, and there are no CCTV cameras around the incident.

The drowsy Electonica gets a lift upon the back of one of her sisters, I cannot tell which one.

The girls sprint over next day. "Mum, we took the day off from sitting in parliament. Besides, when we made a brief appearance in the chamber, all the other members were asleep and snoring. One guy even had a mouse nibbling the food scraps off his beard. We won't be missed."

"Girls, your stepdad wants to conduct a little experiment to determine what part of the avocado fruit is hallucinogenic to Authenticans and which you should avoid. Jules has made the roster up, though the sample size is small, and it may not be valid."

"Go for it, Mum, we're starting to get into this science stuff."

"Jules, just in case, have you got the anti-psychotic drugs handy?" Andromeda asks.

"No, I used them all up," I reply.

I start the instructions:

"Electronica, you eat this avocado fruit skin. It may not be tasty, but you gobbled up my avocado fruit trees before."

"Protonia, you've drawn the lucky straw. You get to eat the yellow flesh of the fruit."

"Neutrnia, you eat the pip, it's full of protein but when I accidentally ate one, once when I was a little bit intoxicated one night and was thinking it was an almond nut, well it didn't taste too good and I had to rush into the garden and fertilize the plants as the toilet bowl was having a malfunction."

"Jules, but what about the avocado tree leaves? The girls ate them too. They should be included in this study."

"Andromeda, you're right. I'll climb up the fence to the next-door neighbour's garden. He's got an Avocado tree and he's away on an island sea cruise at the moment and may not be coming back alive due to this Corona-19++."

"Be careful, Jules."

Andromeda had to rescue me as I got stuck on the top palings of the fence and was screaming in agony as sensitive, down below anatomy parts got crushed but we eventually retrieve some Avocado leaves. Andromeda could just have reached across the fence and saved me a lot of agony, but to her credit, she did get me the ice pack.

"Andromeda, you can eat the Avocado leaves."

"Jules, what are you going to eat?"

"I'm going to be what's called the control group in statistical research. I eat nothing, but I will observe the effects and record them with these cameras and take notes."

And so this monumental, ground-breaking, scientific study begins; maybe a Nobel prize in the making.

Chapter 24

All those scientific tests return negative results for all the girls and Andromeda. It's not the avocados that's causing their strange behaviour, but it may be the shower in the downstairs bathroom. It's full of mould and other creatures that they may be allergic to. Avocados may be safe to eat.

"Girls, use the upstairs bathroom."

They shower and run off to work to join the snoring, bored politicians in parliament.

I wander downstairs, dressed in personal protective equipment (PPE), plus an oxygen tank and mask and holding a scrubbing brush and a 2L bottle of *Pine o Clean*, a disinfectant, and a 2L bottle of bleach. I start furiously scrubbing. I come back upstairs an hour later, looking worse for wear.

"Jules, are you OK?" Andromeda asks.

"Andromeda, the job is done. Can we just lie down?"

"Jules, you smell of bleach and your skin is turning white; can you have a shower in the upstairs bathroom?"

"No, on second thought I got to go to the green grocery store and purchase 6 dozen avocados, limes salt, and 100kg of vegetables but I will shower first so that I don't lose any more of my precious suntan."

"Jules, you can order groceries online and they'll deliver them on their bicycles. Can you also order some squid? I'm feeling kind of peckish."

Ten of those delivery cyclists arrive, their backpacks full of the goodies and they're sweating and panting. I thank them and give a tip, an avocado each but I don't believe they appreciated my tip afterward they gave me the *index finger up* gesture.

"Andromeda, I'll cook the squid with some garlic and avocado on top with vinegar."

"Sounds good to me; make mine a double portion."

A double portion to Authenticans is more like 2 raised to the power of five (32).

After lunch, we do some gardening. Andromeda uses 4 shovels simultaneously. I get sweaty just watching her. The avocado trees seem to be recovering, sprouting new leaves and new banana plants are sprouting from the soil. I'm not slack; I do my bit by planting vegetable seeds into the ground that Andromeda has prepared. I also do the watering with the garden hose though I must admit I added to the nutrient content of the soil when no one was looking. OK, it was just highly nutritious pee with little salt content.

"Jules, what shall we watch on TV?"

There's a knock on the door. I get up to open it. The girls are standing there holding steaming shopping bags. I can smell squid.

"Mum and stepdad, we like, well we like, like have given up the vego thing. What's on TV?"

For a moment, I feel worried. Andromeda must have read my mind. "It's OK, Jules, I'll protect you in case the girls want a midnight snack."

"Darlings, we were going to watch an Earth Canadian series called the *Murdoch Mysteries*."

"Sounds fine to us," they collectively reply. "Are Canadians similar to Authenticans?"

"Similar, but not quite," Andromeda replies.

The girls then flop on the beanbags.

"Get off your backsides. This time you will serve us, and the avocados are fine. A bit of salt and lime juice on mine, along with the squid. Jules likes his squid cooked," Andromeda instructs. The girls jump up and are busy in the kitchen. It doesn't take long when 24 arms work together. They bring out the meals.

"Mum, those people on the TV dress funny and drive strange-looking cars."

"Stop talking, darling, and keep on eating. This is Earth history; the setting is 140 years ago. We have to watch it to learn about this planet and what makes it tick."

Luckily, Andromeda and I did a 7.5 km walk before the girls arrived. I got my 10,000 steps in, though, and Andromeda only got 7,000. She takes bigger foot or arm steps. We had a bit of an argument about that. She said that she has 8 feet against my only two; therefore, her steps should count as

4 times 7,000. Whatever the dubious logic, we deserve a big feed. The video show continues, and we're lying on the bean bags.

"Mum, this is way before they had the hyperdrive."

"Darling, they had bicycles to travel around, and Earth still has them. Space travel on Earth will happen in the 25th century, according to *Star Trek*."

"Stepdad, have you got any more of those avocados?"

Andromeda replies, "Jules, it is OK; you solved the sanitary problem, so let us just let the girls slice up more avocados and limes before the next episode starts."

"Girls, your turn to prepare the snacks, but put the avocado skins and pips in the recycle bin, they are not digestible ot animals and humans," Andromeda says.

"But mum, we need the fibre in our diet."

"Darlings, I am sure Jules does not wish to spend hours unclogging the toilet, so just do as I say."

They shuffle off to the kitchen and soon return with bowls full of peeled, sliced avocado, dipped in apple cider vinegar and Potassium Chloride salt (a salt that doesn't cause heart disease and high blood pressure like Sodium Chloride salt does). If they ever quit their government jobs, they'd be in high demand in the restaurant industry and be paid equivalent wages for 12 staff members, as they have 24 hands working to prepare meals.

It's another late night, and we finish watching the first series, 13 episodes, but only because the girls turned the video player on Fast-forward. They seem to comprehend it. Luckily, I had watched the series before, so I just dozed off as I cannot process information as fast as they do.

Andromeda drags me to our bedroom. "The girls better stay here tonight again. I will get the blankets and cover them and put out a big bowl of squid next to them in case they become peckish during the night."

I feel relieved, though I wonder, what if Earth runs out of squid and avocado?

Chapter 25

Time takes its toll living on Earth; It seems like about 40 years have passed.

Both Andromeda and I still do our nightly walks, but we use walking sticks; only one in my case.

The girls had got the hyperdrive going and journeyed to Authentica, returning with Authentican Octopi-like partners. Protonia gave birth to young, annoying, octopus-looking kids, so we don't see or hear from them that often, apart from delirious phone calls.

"Mum, I can't breastfeed. I have no breasts."

"Put the kids into a blender, sorry I meant squid, not kids into a blender, and then pour the juice into a bottle," Andromeda replies.

Our Earthly squid need to start breeding faster; otherwise, they'll soon become an endangered species, and if that happens, humans may also become an endangered species.

We'll go back in time a little. What else happened? Well, the parliamentary bill the girls put forward and argued for was passed. It was an anti-discrimination bill that made it illegal to discriminate against any living thing that has more than two legs or arms.

The girls ring us on the phone, and Andromeda answers.

"Mum, we don't have to wear the long gowns and veils anymore when we go for a walk, but there are still some humans that yell out wog as they drive past in their hotted-up revving cars."

"Darling, their IQ is probably way below the humankind average, they are called morons on the intelligence scale, just ignore them, but resist chasing their cars and turning them upside down, else you would become as moronic as them. They are just bogans, a species from early human evolution that diverged from the rest of humankind and have never evolved a fully functioning brain."

Wow, what a speech by Andromeda, though I do agree with her sentiments.

"Mum, we hadn't looked up the human meaning of moron and bogan because if we had, we would have never named our about-to-be-born baby daughters Moronica and Boganica, plus we may have multiple births, one after the other."

"Darling, you only name an event after it happens; you jumped the gun, as they call a premature event on Earth. As soon as they are born, you had better rush over to the *Registry of Deaths, Births, and Marriages* and change their future names as quickly as possible."

"Mum, can you think of any alternative names?"

"Darling, if it were a boy, you could call him *Avocado*, which is a tasty Latin American-sounding name, and the girls would love him if he practised the accent, but the girls' names, I have no idea. I have to think, Bananarama; no, on second thought, how about Celery for one of my grand-daughters and Mint for the other."

"Mum, I like those names, they remind me of stepdad's garden. Mum, you had better spend time thinking up more names. I'm in hospital at the moment and my sisters are giving birth as well. You have to come up with at least four more names, actually eight, because we don't know if they're boys or girls. On second thought, at least 64 new names are needed, just in case we have multiple sets of twins, triplets, or quadruplets. We have no idea how many we will give birth to."

"Andromeda, we still have plenty of money left over from the girls' Melbourne Cup winnings. How about we set up a squid farm in Moreton Bay?" I ask.

"Jules, can we buy the whole bay? If our grandkids multiply, we may need more feeding resources."

A song comes on the radio: Paul Kelly – *"From Little Things Big Things Grow."* We love the song, but it doesn't quite fit the current context. I find the CD, I got it, and we play it again, over and over. Then the phone rings again.

"Mum, we're running over with my sisters and our partners. We got the kids in our backpacks. There are quite a few. Can you purchase some squid and avocados? We've slowed down a lot as we've aged; it may take us at least three minutes to get there."

"Jules, what have we got?" Andromeda asks.

"Not enough, but I got a hotline to Harry, and he's now into promoting avocados."

"Sure Jules, a 1000kg all up, 500kg of squid and the rest avocados, but what are you up to?"

"Harry, I have a lot of hungry family to feed, and there's a sort of large family reunion. Can you make it quick?"

"Why don't you just go to those fast-food chains?"

"Harry, it is complicated. Can you just deliver? You got my credit card details."

The kids and grandkids finally arrive. Luckily, they were pulled over for an alcohol random breath test by the police and waited in a long queue. They tested negative, but apparently, the breath-testing device had to be disposed of afterwards, as it was unusable. I'm fortunate to have lost my sense of smell.

I am frantically trying to keep the grandkids from fiddling with my computer and DVD collection. It's a nightmare. I wish they had human development lifecycles and just lie there in a crib for the first 12 months of their lives, but no, these newborns are up and about, crawling around on all eights and fiddling with everything in sight. I need to calm down. I need a drink of wine, actually multiple bottles of wine. Luckily, there is a knock on the door, and the food delivery guys arrive. And so a ravenous food frenzy begins.

"Girls, you've got to teach these grandkids some table manners," I announce.

Electronica comes over, licking her long tongue. Luckily, Andromeda comes over and flings her to the couch.

"Now, girls and boys, what shall we watch? We have over 2000 of these *Star Trek* episodes and movies."

Luckily, I purchased four cartons of crisps the other day, and Andromeda had purchased 12 more beanbags, which also arrived. The girl Octopi and their male partners help me bring the beanbags up from the downstairs garage; well, I just instructed how to unpack them. The bags are all unwrapped and ready to go.

The precocious grandkids are jumping on them. "It's not a trampoline," I yell.

"We want to watch that one, no that one, no that one," the girls argue."

"Shut your faces and chew on the crisps. Your stepdad will decide," Andromeda yells.

I pick the 2030 Star Trek DVD movie. It's called *Close Encounters with Authenticans.*"

Everyone is laughing, including the grandkids. "Jules, they should have checked the facts," one of the girls' partners says.

"Mate, have another beer; it's all a joke, as we say in OZ."

They leave after the movie, waving goodbye and smiling as they run off. I look at the trail of destruction in the lounge room and start putting my DVDs back into their covers, then start furiously vacuuming the pieces of crisps and squid lying on the floor.

Andromeda puts several arms around me. "Jules, there will always be some compromises when you have kids and grandkids; stop being so pedantic."

I give her a kiss, but I definitely hope not to live to the time when there are great-great-grandkids.

Andromeda is searching my precious DVD collection.

"Jules, how about we put on this DVD; it is called *Grumpy Old Men.*

Chapter 26

I'm furiously drilling and screwing locks on every cabinet in the house.

"Andromeda, these are the keys, and I've labelled all 65 of them, and next time the grandkids are here, I don't want any of the dinner plates used as Frisbees and going through the glass windows."

"Jules, settle down, you know I'll always help to clean up the mess and glass."

I'm sweating and puffing.

"Jules, you may have to watch that grumpy movie again. No, on second thought, let us go for a walk. You will let off some steam, and then we can watch the movie again afterwards. I will race you, Jules."

I decline the offer. I know I haven't got a chance. She has four walking sticks to my two.

The grandkids grow up very quickly. Four years have passed, and the grandkids are now polite and well-mannered and are no longer weapons of mass destruction.

"Jules, I have just had a phone call; they are all running over soon. Can you ring Harry's son and order 2000kg of squid and 500 avocados?"

I do that.

The grandkids rush out to the delivery semi-trailer, bringing the goodies in from the truck and honing in on the food along with their parents. I'm the only one who likes my squid cooked, so I wait for the microwave oven to finish. An hour later, after some conversation whilst gorging ourselves, we all try to squeeze onto the 12 beanbags. I whisper to

Andromeda, "We've got to buy more beanbags", as I'm lying on the hard floor. Later, Andromeda slithers over, and then she asks, "Jules, have you made a Will, in case you die and the assets have to be distributed?"

That's got me worried. "No, I haven't."

"Jules, you never know when your last day on Earth may be."

I turn on the 3D streaming device. "What shall we watch?" I ask Andromeda.

"What about this old TV series, *Death in Paradise?* There are hundreds of episodes." The kids and grandkids refrain from complaining. They see the previews.

"Grand stepdad, we would love to live on one of those Caribbean islands," one of them calls out. Don't know which grandkid, and I can't even remember all their names, as they all look the same to me. I look at Andromeda.

"Jules sounds good, but we have to look at the Caribbean islands at their non-human rights records. I don't want my grandkids ending up on a BBQ."

I reflect on the racial and sexual atrocities committed in the 2020s and a very long way before that. Things are a bit better now, thanks to my stepdaughters. I cautiously walk towards them, all 3 of them. They hug me with very many arms. "Stepdad, we won't eat you, and we have only good memories of you. We are going back. We could find oxygen-generating equipment so you could live on Authentica, though you may appear a bit weird or an amputee with only two arms if you come with us. You could be discriminated against, but we'd like to do our best to prevent that happening."

I look at Andromeda, "What do you think?"

"Jules, there are many chemical compounds on Authentica that have lots of oxygen. We have the technology to extract oxygen, which we never needed to use. This could be a first, and we can always come back if you do not like it, but Jules, pay off your credit card debt before we go."

"Girls, partners, and grandchildren," Andromeda announces very loudly, "You have to notify the authorities here that you are leaving. Otherwise, the police will think you have been killed or abducted, and a search and rescue squad will look for you and question Jules and me as we are next of kin. We will be suspects in your disappearance, as many disappearances are caused by those known to the victim on this planet."

I butt in, "Girls, even moving interstate or a different country is complex on Earth. You have houses, you have jobs, you have bills, you have furniture and beanbags, plus I bet they don't have potato crisps on Authentica."

Andromeda intercedes, "Girls, initially go for a brief holiday to Authentica. We will check on your houses and empty the letterboxes. Places change, and Authentica may be different now; check it out thoroughly before you move there permanently."

Andromeda looks at me sternly and whispers, "Do not ever put on that *Rocky Horror Picture Show* video again when the kids are here; it has given the girls delusional ideas again. Jules, our cities were built in the oceans. The landmasses, well, the landscape was barren. I do not know if bananas or avocados could grow there, but I did dig up some banana rhizomes and kept some avocado pips. The girls will take them on their holiday and plant them on any land mass on Authentica; it is an experiment, Jules."

"Andromeda, there are all these laws that we can't introduce foreign species into alien cultures, else we may contaminate them."

"Jules, come over here." She gives me a kiss. "Jules, you have been contaminated since you joined that alien dating site. Those well-paid anthropologists are the only guys worried about contamination so that they can do their studies on the origin of species. It is all rhetoric, and most species are resilient and adept, though those magnificent dinosaurs you had on Earth were not, and our species did not kill them. Can we watch a dinosaur movie?"

She continues, "Time passes differently on Authentica, as it is so close to a very strong gravitational field from its red dwarf, shrinking sun, which makes time slow down relative to Earth time. Since Authentica has a highly elliptical orbit, time can speed up at times. The planet goes around its sun every 200 Earth seconds, though we do not feel it. According to that guy Einstein, time should slow down on our world, but it is the opposite. It speeds up in terms of birthdays. We have a birthday every 200 seconds, and we can barely keep up shopping for birthday presents, attending birthday parties, and funerals."

Now, I think I know why they can run so fast on Earth. A week later, the girls, their partners, and their kids come running back to visit.

"It's all done, mum; we rented the houses out, but can you collect the rent and pay the council rates and any other bills in case we decide to stay on Authentica."

What are kids for, I wonder?

"Andromeda, we can do a brief visit, an Authentican week at most".

"Jules, I said before, time moves differently in our world, but at least you will not become any more decrepit in an Authentican week, but you better pay all the bills and rates for at least 1 year in advance."

"Now darlings, enjoy your holiday and be back soon to finalise all the paperwork if you decide to go back permanently. I have set the hyperdrive to return here automatically in 8 Earthian days; it is like a homing pigeon; Earth is now its home."

The girls nod their heads, and they, along with their partners and kids, enter the refrigerator-like hyperdrive. The body shrinker must have been fixed as they all fitted in. The drive vanishes.

I pack my favourite DVD collection and photos, just the important things. The photos are the most important thing you can take with you. I watched as the girls and grandkids prepared for the ride.

"The hyperdrive is the size of a fridge," I ask Andromeda. "How can they all fit in?"

"Jules, I fixed the compressor; as they walk in, one at a time, it compresses them to the size of your toenail and decompresses them on arrival. It can carry thousands of toenails."

"Mum, it's not working."

"Darling, just press the ON button, it is like a microwave oven. It will get the hyperdrive going, but enter the coordinates first."

Unfortunately, the hyperdrive does not produce the whizzy noises that the *Doctor Who* phone box makes when it takes off. They're all off without a whisper.

A peaceful week on Earth passes.

"Andromeda, how about we watch the 50th TV series of *Doctor Who*?"

"Jules, they were supposed to end it after series 13. The Doctor was supposed to have only 13 reincarnations, and this is series 50?"

"Andromeda, I think they may have got the maths wrong and left out a trailing zero."

We hug on the beanbags, and I stream the latest episode of *Doctor Who*.

"Jules, what's going on? Our daughters are in the new *Doctor Who* episode even though they are far, far away." Andromeda was wrong. The hyperdrive suddenly materialises in our kitchen. The hyperdrive must have the hots for my kitchen fridge. The girls, their partners, and their kids walk out in turns.

"Mum and stepdad, we're back. In one week, we spent the equivalent of 200 years on Earth. It was a bit boring. All the girls, partners and grandkids nod their heads in agreement. We'll tell you the story later. These are the compressed food packs; they should decompress. If they don't, phone Harry's son and make a food order. We are super hungry. It's like we haven't eaten in 200 years or more. We could even eat stepdad if he showers when he comes out of the toilet."

Protonia continues, "Oh, and mum, can we all stay at your and stepdad's house for three months? We rented our houses out for 3 Earth year months, and we have nowhere to stay," she says in a tearful type of voice whilst bowing her head in sorrow and wiping tears from 4 eyes.

Andromeda looks at me. I nod my head to indicate a *yes*. I don't think I had much choice.

"All my darlings, you can stay, but all 12 of you have to share that big room downstairs."

"Mum, that would be like, like being in a refugee camp, plus it's got no beds or curtains," Electronica says with a tinge of disgust in her voice.

I interrupt, "Guys, here's the phone. You can ring that *Herman Norman* department store and order what you need. Tonight, you'll have to sleep on the bean bags in the lounge, otherwise in the garden, and you have to do house chores and contribute to the food bills."

They all look at each other in amazement and bewilderment, but finally, with less than happy looks, eventually nod their heads in agreement.

Andromeda whispers to me, "Jules, you were so forceful; here are your blood-pressure tablets."

Next day, a truck delivers 12 more beanbag coverings and plastic bags full of polystyrene balls. I show them how to fill the bags without making too much of a mess. I can hear sounds of laughter from the stairwell.

"Jules, we may have to postpone that holiday on Authentica for at least three months."

"Andromeda, I'm so deeply disappointed. I was so looking forward to being under the sea in an *Octopus's Garden*." I lied. I never wanted to go there anyway. I wouldn't fit in unless I had cosmetic surgery to give me more limbs.

We're lying in bed. "Jules, your sentiments are so translucent, you cannot lie to me."

I think she meant transparent, but I won't correct her.

She wraps her eight arms around me. "We will cope," she says.

Next day, we hear the story of what the exoplanet Authentica is really like now, after millions of 200-second years.

Chapter 27

They all come upstairs after a good night's sleep.

"Mum, stepdad, we have to run to that container storage place where we put all our essential goods—our clothing and the kids' school uniforms. The school holidays finish tomorrow.

"Of course, darlings, Jules and I will look after your kids.

"Jules, you have that ancient board game called Chess. Teach the juniors how to play it. It will keep them occupied."

I do that. It's not long before they pick up on the strategies, and five minutes later, I'm checkmated. They learned quickly, but there were six of them. I'm not giving up. Our next game of chess will be one-on-one with aluminium foil over our heads, just in case they transmit some sort of telepathic cues to each other.

The girls and their partners arrive carrying many boxes.

"Mum, stepdad, can you keep the kids entertained for another 20 minutes? We have more stuff to purchase, and we can't run as fast as we used to."

"Sure darlings, Jules will take them down to the local school's tennis courts and show them how to play tennis."

That was an even worse idea. All three of my tennis racquets are ruined. They served at least 300km per hour and punctured all the strings. Then again, they could possibly win a Grand Slam, which could be good, as our finances are getting a bit low, due to the monstrous food bills, and I'm sure we can purchase new racquets with steel or titanium strings.

Andromeda slithers over to me. "Jules, what about that game called *Dominoes*, not the pizza place, but a game with rectangular blocks with white dots on them? I checked all your belongings, including the boxes labelled *Do Not Touch*. I did investigate and found that you have a dominoes set along with many board games that, judging by their condition, you may have played them with your father when you were young."

"Grandkids, can you Google the game called *Dominoes*? I've long forgotten how to play that game."

At least their minds are occupied.

"Grand-step-granddad, you cheated. You distracted us with those potato crisps."

I sure did and won as I raised my hands in glory. "I'm the new Domino's champion."

Andromeda comes over to me. "Jules, it's not about winning unless you have some severe psychological disorder or have a huge financial gain to make. Come over here, "You and your grandkids don't have to win every time. You can have a draw or a deadlock."

She continues, "The inhabitants of your planet have some morbid desire to win and dominate; that is why there are wars, power struggles, flaunting wealth and gambling problems on this planet."

She's so very right.

"Jules, what about this game from your game box? It is called *Snakes and Ladders* and is totally based on random dice throws, like those games your people play at casinos. It will not teach them competitive strategies. It is just about fun."

"Andromeda, you're right again, but can we have a practice game without the grandkids? Plus, I'm feeling a bit peckish, and crisps don't satisfy my hunger. I've got a craving. Can we walk down to the corner store and get some sweets, some of those chocolate-covered *Martian* bars?"

"Jules, you will develop type 2 diabetes. They are full of sugar. At our age, we have to stay away from sweet things."

I don't comment. The girls and their partners finish unpacking all their necessary belongings. Luckily, I have a huge wardrobe and cupboards downstairs to which I give them the keys.

"Stepdad, you have to be joking. Can you remove the locks?"

"Here's the battery-powered drill and the screw-driver bit heads. It works in reverse as well. I'm sure you'll work out how to use this primitive device to remove the locks."

There's a lot of noise and arguing coming from downstairs.

"Jules, let them work it out. The damage to your furniture will probably be minimal, and I know you are worried about the fate of that drill you have owned for over 30 years. You have a lot of attachment to that tool."

"Andromeda, the way you use the English language is highly inappropriate and can be misinterpreted."

"Jules, that depends on the way your mind thinks; you seem highly sexually frustrated. You can hire an Earthling mistress if you like, but I will watch you both to gain some tips."

"I won't do that. There's this Internet site called *somthingnaughtyhub* where I can get my hormonal satisfaction," I reply.

"Jules, can I watch what you are watching, as the grandkids and their parents are downstairs?"

I turn the computer on and log onto the website.

"Jules, my hormones are out of control. Keep that video on. It might give you some ideas on how to satisfy an alien partner."

In the background, an ancient song is playing on the radio: Stevie Nicks' "*Age of 17.*"

Andromeda is salivating. I think briefly, you either run away or take another chance.

I ring Harry's son, the now delivery guy, and also call Harry. Some parents just lack imagination in naming their kids.

"Harry Junior, four dozen red roses, please."

"By the way, Andromeda, what did the girls name their kids?"

"Jules, they chose to keep it simple: the numbers from one to six in order of birth."

"So, which one is numero uno?"

"One, of course."

"But they all look the same to me. I'll get some string and cardboard. I'll make name tags, which hopefully they'll wear."

"Jules, their personalities are subtly different. In time, you will see that and forget about the name tags; they will swap them around to get a laugh at your expense, as my daughters did."

The bunch of roses are delivered.

"Oh, thanks, Jules, they taste wonderful."

Vases, that's other things I can get rid of, as we downsize on belongings in our old age.

Chapter 28

The girls, partners and kids descend the stairs.

"Mum, we're going for a short 30km run. We won't be long. Do you want to join us?

Stepdad, you can join us too, and if you have a cardio incident, we can give you mouth-to-mouth resuscitation and carry you to the hospital afterwards."

I politely decline the offer, but Andromeda accepts the challenge.

"Look after my walking sticks," she says to me.

I'm worried and chewing my fingernails and toenails, hoping Andromeda will cope, but 240 seconds later, they arrive back. Andromeda won the race. I give her a hug which was a mistake; should have waited till she took a shower and rinsed her mouth. One thing to note, the breath of an Authentican, after they've eaten food or indulged in heavy exercise, is better than a defibrillator device at reviving a heart that's gone into fibrillation.

I guess the walking sticks were only a ploy to get me outside, and to think I only used my walking stick to get Andromeda outside, definitely a communication failure.

"Mum, I don't know how you did it, but Mum and Stepdad, we have to go to work. There is a sitting of Parliament today, and our partners are returning to their jobs in Community Services. They do have showers in the buildings, and we always carry industrial-strength deodorants."

"Stepdad, can you drive the kids to school? I don't want them to run without adult supervision, plus they may not have student showers at primary schools, so they'd better shower here."

"Electronica, Neutronica, and Protonica, I asked you to wear name tags so I know who I'm talking to, but yes, I will drive you to school. You know, most primary schools have after-school care centres."

Andromeda gives me a thump in the ribs and says, "Of course, darlings, Jules will also pick them up and bring them back to our home; after all, what are grandparents for?"

"Andromeda, when the girls return to their houses, how about we go to Disney World in the USA? I've never been there."

"Jules, read the newspapers. Those southern states of the USA are so full of racial discrimination and violence. I would be roasted alive and turned into Octopus rings. Think of another destination."

I'm researching. "How about a place that has a great waterslide in Bali; my ex-wife and I had a great time there climbing up and slithering down."

"Jules, you never told me you were once married."

"Andromeda, you never asked, though you did mention your 10 or 12 Authentican ex-husbands."

"Jules, in those old days, we consumed the male partners after the mating ritual. That has now been banned on Authentica, as according to the girls, the population is still dwindling, so males are now a protected species, kept in secure cages, and only used for breeding purposes by extracting their sperm with needles and using what you call IVF."

Oh, God, I don't think a holiday to Authentica would be a good idea. The Water Slides on Earth are definitely safer.

"Andromeda, after we finish this 3-month stint with the grandkids, we'll go water-sliding."

"Jules, we can do it, but what if the grandkids want to come along?"

I cringe. "Andromeda, they'd take up at least two plane seats each. Our finances are stretching."

"Jules, we will swim there, probably get there quicker than the plane, and have some good feeds along the way."

"Have you got passports?"

"Jules, no, and there are no border checks when you climb out of the ocean, so we will bring swimsuits and clothing with us and generally keep a low profile so as to fit in."

I guess we'll have to break into the water park after dark. I'm sure the grandkids can disable security and get the water slide pumps going.

"OK, Andromeda, we'll do it, but I'll catch a plane."

"Jules, we can make another harness and you can ride on my back again. It will not be that uncomfortable unless there is a sea storm by the seashore. You have done it before when you were younger."

Horrible images flood my mind - riding on Andromeda's back and trying to get a breath when she surfaces amidst the waves.

"I'll catch the plane and meet you there; I'll give you the coordinates of the resort," I say.

"Jules, it is still 2.5 months away till the next school holidays. You have plenty of time to think, but I want to know more about your previous marriage partner and your relationship."

"I'll try to arrange a meeting of the three of us. There are always two sides to a story. You can always be an independent adjudicator. I can give my side of the story, but it may be biased."

"Jules, it is not a court of law, and I cannot be independent, but do you still love her?"

"You mean my ex-wife. I've moved on, though I still care for her."

I grab Andromeda, "I now love you predominantly."

"Jules, can you be more romantic and less clinical? I will not ask about your previous relationships again."

"And I won't ask about yours, but you do sometimes mumble in your sleep. You once said the husband ten was the yummiest. I had night terrors for months afterwards after hearing that."

We're cuddling, and a song comes on the radio, *Sophie B. Hawkins - As I Lay Me Down.*

I turn on the computer, go to YouTube, and find another song by the same artist called *Right Beside You*.

"Do you find that attractive singer/writer beautiful?"

"I do, but I find many people and things beautiful, even those paintings hanging on the walls of our house."

"Jules, you called it our house."

"It is our house, and don't ask me again if I made a Will; you'll get it if I pass away before you."

"Jules, I do not want it; in your Will, you can donate it to charity."

For a moment, I think about that guy whose company is named after a river in South America, and he aspires to be the world's wealthiest man, but isn't noted as donating much to charity. Money is useless when you're dead.

"Oh sh*t, it's 3:00 pm. I got to pick up the grandkids from primary school. Where are the keys to the van?"

"Jules, they are on that chain you wear around your neck."

I kiss her. "Andromeda, I love you. Can you ring Harry2 and order more food?"

I'm struggling to get the van started. Andromeda slithers over, "Jules, this is where the key goes."

Chapter 29

It's a Sunday morning, and we're all sitting in the lounge room.

Andromeda says, "Girls, it's time you tell us what happened in Authentica when you went back for your holiday."

"Mum, we mentioned before that it has changed, not just the planet but the inhabitants. They are becoming greedy."

"Tell me more, darlings."

"Mum, some of the inhabitants were hoarding squid and selling them at very inflated prices. The oceans are almost depleted of squid. That's why we girls, our partners, and kids lost so much weight. We could only afford to eat one meal a day instead of six. And mum, some of them now aspire to be billionaires, whilst others starve. It's not the same as it used to be when we all worked for the good of the whole community."

I look at Andromeda, and she whispers in my ear. "Jules, our race was very technologically developed but also agrarian, or should I say waterian, and we never really had the concept of ownership when I was there last. We did not even have the concept of money. We got bonus points in the halls of fame for being generous."

I'm wondering if greed is something that evolves in a society, and if so, why? You can't take your fortune with you when you die unless there are heaven or hell credit points.

"The same thing happened on Earth and is still happening. You beat us on the technology front, but we came way ahead on greed," I announce.

"Jules and Mum, before we had a collective ego. We did what was good for our whole society. That collective ego is disappearing on our planet."

Andromeda slithers over to them all and gives them a hug.

"Mum, we've all decided to stay on Earth, plus the babysitting service is great here," Neutronica says with a wicked smile.

"Jules, book that holiday to the Caribbean for all of us after the next Melbourne Cup race," Andromeda instructs. Booking a holiday is something I guess I have to learn how to do.

"Andromeda, are you going to run?" I ask.

"Jules, I'll go slowly and only win by a head, so as not to arouse suspicion. Have we still got those horse costumes?"

Chapter 30

"Andromeda, you don't have to run in the Melbourne Cup. We still have most of those giant gold wedding rings you wore on each arm from your previous husbands. There are at least 100kg of gold, which, unlike on your planet, is worth a lot on Earth. We can sell some of the gold and go on that holiday."

The girls intervene. "Mum, stepdad, we earn plenty of money for doing very little in our government jobs. We'll pay for the holiday to the Caribbean, and we'll also pay for all food consumed in this household, which has been mainly by us and our families. We've contacted Harry-Junior, and all your food expenses will be billed to us. You don't have to earn money by racing and risking injury."

For a second, I reflect. The girls think as one, with no sibling rivalry. They even talk at the same time, saying the same thing in perfect synchronicity. They think and work as a collective.

"Thank you, darlings, but I want to run just to prove I am not old and decrepit."

"Mum, you have nothing to prove. If you want, we can all have another 30km race again if it makes you feel better."

Needless to say, after much sewing and knitting to expand the horse costume, Andromeda effortlessly won the Cup. The real horses were really pissed off, shaking their heads in disbelief, but we got the money, honey.

A few months have passed, and now we're sitting on some Caribbean Island, sipping champagne while the grandkids are diving in the waters and catching a feed. We look at the red sunset.

"Partners, get the kids. We've all got to look at this red sunset," Andromeda yells out. The male Authenticans oblige. We're sitting on the beach watching the sunset. It seems like the Authentican females, like Hyenas on Earth, are the dominant gender, which is OK with me. I can just relax and sip a beer or champagne whilst she does all the holiday organising, house cleaning, paying bills, and looking after the grandkids; life is good.

"Jules, our sunsets lasted microseconds every 57 seconds. This is nice. How long do you think your sun will last, and will your planet get soaked up by your sun?"

"Andromeda, I've read that we have 4 billion years left before we have to start worrying about that. It's highly likely our Earthly species will exterminate itself way, way before that time. Unfortunately, our Earthly species is driven by male egos that basically have problems with their egos and believe that dominating and overpowering others will give them some satisfaction, which they lack from maybe a financially rich but neglected childhood. They need praise from their constituents. Most of our problems on Earth are due to insatiable male egos who rule the countries here."

"Jules, you are preaching again; maybe you should enter politics and set them straight."

"I'm too old, but I'll keep on writing."

"Let me hold your head, Jules, and sing you a song."

"Jules, your species may turn things around. When we get home, can we watch some of your hippy videos? Now smoke this. It may make you feel better."

And so dear readers, the story kind of ends. It's a hippy ending, sorry, I meant a happy ending.

I lie next to Andromeda and embrace her with my two arms. She reciprocates but with all eight arms. I've gotten used to the choke hold.

"I love you," I whisper.

"I love you, too, and I promise I will never eat you," she whispers back.

I get prodded. I look up. It's a nurse.

"Sir, you've spent 30 hours in REM dreaming sleep according to the electrodes placed around your head. That is highly unusual as a sleep cycle doesn't normally last longer than 90 minutes, and only around 15 minutes of dreaming sleep in each cycle. You were also talking in your sleep about an Andromeda and Octopi. You must take the medication you were put on to bring you back to normal, and be careful when mopping the kitchen floor. We have to care for senior citizens like you who slip, fall, and hit their heads all the time. You're a lucky man, though there was a tall, unusually dressed person with a veil covering much of her face attending and holding your hand. She wouldn't say her name."

"No nurse, if it was a dream, it was the most awesome dream you could ever imagine. Forget the medication; I just want to go back to sleep and keep on dreaming. It was a great dream."

"OK, I will discharge you from protected care as long as you sign this patient non-liability, non-confidentiality, non-retraction, dismissal agreement."

I quickly do that.

As I stagger out of the Royal Brisbane Hospital, rubbing my eyes, a fridge-like device appears in front of me, and the door opens.

"Hop in quickly," she says. "*Star Trek Enterprise* is about to start on your Earthian TV channel, and the grandkids are starving."

"I'm so glad you're here," I whisper.

Embracing was a big mistake; it distracted Andromeda, and we crashed on Earth's moon, right on the 100kg of excrement and other junk that Neil Armstrong and Buzz Aldrin left when Earthians first visited there in 1969. They sure must have eaten a lot.

"Andromeda, call the girls. I can't breathe here and don't open the door."

"Here, take this oxygen-producing tablet. You may feel bloated, but it works. The girls have purchased a new hyperdrive from that *Jay-Bee High Fly* store. They'll be here any minute."

"Mum, can you and stepdad get out and walk at least 100 metres whilst we disinfect you guys? And stepdad, take those soiled shoes off and leave them next to the poo bags you stepped on and punctured. You'd be contaminating the universe, plus we don't want to spend hours cleaning the inside of our new, beautiful hyperdrive."

"Jules, you only have a few minutes before your body explodes due to the lack of atmospheric pressure that was holding you together, according to that *Arnold* movie, *Total Recall*. Now move it.

We've cleaned up and made it inside the girls' hyperdrive refrigerator-like device, and my eyeballs haven't popped out like in the movie.

And so what happened?

We outbid property developers and purchased a retirement village that was going to be demolished to make way for high-rise apartments. As the village residents passed away due to natural causes, the girls and their husbands and kids moved into the apartments. We all get together and have a squid BBQ daily.

"Andromeda, I can't believe this is real. I've been so lucky."

"I cannot either, Jules, but let us enjoy our dreams, give me a hug."

I wake up hugging a pillow, no Andromeda in sight. Maybe it was just a pleasant dream. I stumble to the kitchen, rubbing my head. There is a note by the coffee machine.

The note reads, Jules, I have to briefly return to Authentica for medical treatment. One of my hearts is failing. The daughters, partners and grandkids are taking me back in the hyperdrive. I did not want to distress you, so I did not wake you. I do hope I will be back by the time you wake up.

I'm pacing up and down the lounge, holding my head. I'm more than just severely distressed and about to have a cardiac event myself. Then the fridge device materialises and they all step out - Andromeda, stepdaughters, and step-grandkids.

"Jules, I've been treated. My other heart is working perfectly. I thought you would still be asleep when I returned. I told you before that time operates differently on our planet. I spent 2 months in what you call a hospital. I am like you now; I have only one heart."

I grab her and finally find where to kiss her, "I'm so glad you're back. I woke up too early." Tears are pouring down my face. "My one heart is for you only."

She replies, "With one heart only, I've got to stick with you."

An old song comes on the radio, *If I had a Hammer* by a guy called *Trini Lopez*. We're all dancing, all of us, and put the song on and on again. Andromeda whispers, "How much of that stuff have you smoked?"

"I haven't touched the stuff (I lied and quickly tossed the stash into the organic recycle bin; the worms will be off their heads and probably also writhing to the music); I'm more than happy with reality".

We keep on dancing for many hours. It must have been worth more than a 20km run and at least 30,000 steps. I take the step-grandkids to bed. The stepsisters and their partners are lying on the bean bags in what I assume is a state of sleep.

Andromeda asks me, "Has it all been worth it?"

I wrap my arms around her, "It sure has, couldn't be better".

"Jules, you have not had a shower after all that aromatic sweaty dancing. Hop into the bathroom. I'll join you and wrap my arms around you."

I open my eyes. Where's Andromeda? All I see is a blurred image of a nurse frantically shaking my shoulders and then thumping my chest whilst another nurse applies a re-breather facemask and is yelling for a doctor or surgeon. This can't be real. It's a repeat of me waking up in hospital once before after hitting my head in a fall. Andromeda came to visit and took me back home, but I look around, there is no Andromeda.

"He's stabilizing; his heart rate is nearly back to earthling normal, and so is his blood pressure. I have no idea what could have caused such a serious cardio reaction in someone so young. He looks like he's in his early thirties. He has two skin puncture marks on his body, but check his blood for foreign substances like hallucinogens, as we're getting a lot of cases like him who overdosed, so keep him hooked up to all the diagnostic meters for the next 24 hours."

I lift my chest and yell, "It wasn't a dream, if it was, it was the best dream you could ever have!"

"Quiet, sir, this shot will calm you down."

I'm drifting back into unconsciousness, but before I do, a projection of Andromeda appears in my mind. "Jules, we had to leave Earth; my daughters and their partners were continually interrogated about the technology that brought us here. The daughters were even put into custody by a right-wing political government. Fortunately, they had no difficulty bending the prison bars and escaping at very high speed. Your Earthian societies have not been exposed to our technology, as your planet could very much abuse those technologies and use them as weapons of mass destruction. Jules, I love you and will miss you so very, very much."

"Take me with you; I'll somehow adjust to the low oxygen on your planet or bring oxygen tanks with me," I yell out.

"Jules, there is much more you would have to adjust to. I crashed landed on your planet and adjusted the spacecraft's physical metamorphosis device to appear like citizens of your planet and behave like them, but something must have gone very wrong as I did not expect to look as an Octopus-like creature and that hyperdrive fault never was corrected, probably just as well for when my daughters arrived. Jules, without using projections and altering your perception of us physically, we resemble one of your spider species in appearance, but your spiders are very primitive, whereas we are very advanced and large."

"Andromeda, can you keep this fantasy alive?"

"I was joking Jules. I look the same as I always have, and I do project an illusion, but I am happy you like it.

"Andromeda, did you take me for what is called a ride, something which is a deceitful act?"

"Jules, that was never my intention to take you for what you call a ride, but somehow, your perception and observation of time were altered by my intrusion into your life. Much of it was your imagination, that included a sense of adventure that was never satisfied in your real life. However, I admit that I did not try to encourage you to see our relationship objectively. I enjoyed being part of your fantasy, and I am sure my daughters and their offspring did as well. And Jules, only a month has passed in your Earth time for you, though it may appear we spent decades together. We studied your society and your politics. We prefer to invade a more friendly planet rather than one that has never evolved beyond constant wars."

My head is spinning, and I'm wondering if I'm having some sort of psychotic breakdown, and this Andromeda story is just some strange delusion and not reality at all. I call for the doctor, who arrives heavily clad, with only his two eyes being visible.

"Doctor, I think I may be having a psychotic episode due to ingesting too many magic mushrooms on one or maybe three occasions in my life. Nothing makes sense, though I hallucinated a most wonderful dream that is sort of ending. Can you administer an anti-psychotic drug to me?"

"Nurse, give him the oxygen mask and keep it on till I find the oxygen pills."

I raise my head. Several over seven-foot-tall, hairy spider-like creatures are standing on a few hind legs and securing a mask over my face. I'm terrified, super, super terrified, but then I hear a familiar voice from one of the spider creatures, "Jules, everything will be all right. I have had a type of house built suitable for two-legged creatures and equipped with oxygen pumps. You will be able to wander around the house without any breathing apparatus, and I can always put the projection into effect so that you can find my Octopusy body attractive rather than my true spider body.

I'm back in total confusion; it's a nightmare, and I'm frantically tossing my head from left to right whilst tied down on what must be a hospital stretcher.

I vaguely hear, "He is not ready to move to our world; his mind would collapse more than it is now doing."

I try to focus and look up. A spider-like creature is caressing my forehead. I put my hand in my mouth and refrain from screaming. It then appears to turn into the Octopus-like creature, Andromeda, that I got used to, cherished in my life, and even loved.

"Andromeda, is any of this real?"

"Jules, reality and time are very subjective concepts; not everyone in the Universe experiences them in the same way, and it depends on how close you live near a high gravity source. Time can go off in what you call tangents."

"Andromeda, are you really here as Spiderwoman?"

"Ha, ha, let me give you a hug."

I close my eyes, and then I wake up. I'm lying with my headphones surrounding my head. A song is playing by a group called *Lastlings*—"*Take My Hand*." I relate to it.

Then I hear, "I have to go back to my planet. I hope you can bring some of those insects you call flies, if you ever visit. I may be a spider woman, but I love you, and you are not on my menu."

I rub my head, exhausted and unable to make it to the bed, so I'm lying on the floor. It must have all been a drug-induced incident, though I haven't touched hallucinogens for over 15 years and have not taken any other substance. Then a 3D image, photoshoot type, materializes in my lounge; it's Andromeda and her family waving their hands, Octopi hands.

I yell out, "I can handle the spiders. Show me the real picture; do it, Andromeda!"

"Jules, you are a very persuasive male specimen of your Earthian species, and I did love to be with you."

"Andromeda, would I have to be surgically modified to look like a spider?"

"No, Jules. You would make a good museum exhibit. I would take you home at night, which is very frequent on our planet. I promise I will not eat you," the spider image of Andromeda says while licking her tongue.

I can't finish the story, but I think I may have been teleported. I look up. Andromeda is flashing and trying to stabilize a flashing image between the octopus-like image of her and the spider image. It takes some time—microseconds, seconds, hours—who knows, as time works differently when near high gravitational fields; it slows down. She puts some sort of breathing device in my mouth.

"Keep it in your mouth till I find another way to compensate for our low oxygen levels."

"Whatever you are, we had a good time together, and I love you and would like to stay." A song comes on radio, *Mary in the Morning*. It induces lots of tears in me and tears in her, which fall on my face. She then hugs me with all eight arms, and our tears connect and unite.

"Jules, my tears will convert your body to one of our species, and you will live thousands of years, be it short years, and you will not need an oxygen mask. You will be one of us, my SpiderMan partner, and I promise you will not be consumed by anyone except me," SpiderWoman laughs.

Sorry, have no time to finish the story as a day goes by on this planet by the time I finish a single sentence. But overall,

I'm really happy being with Andromeda or Spiderwoman, as I now call her.

Anyway, have fun whatever space you might be in, whether in your mind or in the Andromedian universe.

Very kind regards from,

Spiderwoman and Spiderman

www.ingramcontent.com/pod-product-compliance
Lightning Source LLC
Chambersburg PA
CBHW051258170626
46809CB00004B/1713